Tears Of A True Hustler

Simone Majors

DEDICATION

This book is dedicated to women who had no choice but to live a hard life style such as the character Krazy. Beneath that hard skin there is still a warm heart and soul and I hope this book as well as this series inspire you women to seek better and rise above whatever is going on in your life. This book is dedicated to the young ladies who think that a man should love you because you his "Down Bitch." I hope this series is an eye opener for you young women to choose a different lifestyle and be all you can be. I hope this book inspire all the women and men out there that have a dream of being an author. I hope that every single one of you enjoy my book " Tears of a True Hustler" and be on the lookout for more projects from me!!!!!

- Simone Majors

CONTENTS

ACKNOWLEDGMENTS

I would like to acknowledge God for giving me this gift of creativity to be able to write this book. I would like to give a shout out to my wonderful publisher, you are more than a publisher you are my best friend and someone I can forever lean on! I also want to thank my family The Wiley's and the Krisel's for pushing me and for being a listening ear when I wanted to give up. And also my son, you're the reason why I push myself daily to be all I can be, without you I don't know where I would be in life. I want you to always see that your mother worked hard and made things happen. I love you all and the best is yet to come!

-Simone Majors

Published by Mahogany Publications
www.mahoganypublications.com

Prologue

Before my late husband Jake, there was my young love Kris, but while Kris and Smooth took their leave to Atlanta this man stepped into my world and turned it upside down. What was wrong was now oh so right. My outlook on the world changed in moments when he entered my life. He was and forever will be my ride or die, and my right hand in crime. Everyone has their secrets and this was mine; I fell in love with a man that wasn't truly my own.

All I could hear was the clatter of footsteps rushing across the basement level of the sky rise building which was once known as the base of the notorious crew "The Street Legends." I sat there catching my breath as I heard the police sergeant yell "Put your hands up where we can see them!" I looked through the crack of the crates and boxes only to see the man that had stolen my heart drop to his knees and raise up his arms in defeat. How did all this come to this moment? Tears streamed down my face as I clenched my necklace. My heart was filled with so much pain and agony.

Everything that we had strategically planned had fallen to shambles. It was always said that if you enter this lifestyle there are only two ways out, either in cuffs or in a body bag. But what if this lifestyle is all you know? This is a question that all hustlers have asked themselves one time or another, but during moments like these you will see......TEARS OF A TRUE HUSTLER

CHAPTER 1: HOW IT ALL BEGAN

I knew Kris ever since I was one-years-old. We both lived next door to each other so his family was like my family. Yet, that all changed when we turned eleven.

There was a big time drug lord who came to the area and would always give our parents drugs. He told them that these drugs would calm their nerves, relieving them from the stress that living in the hood would cause.

Little did they know, they were his lab rats, which he used to experiment on with his new concoctions of different drugs? He would mix cocaine and crystal meth, making it so powerful that they would lose their minds. Which they did! Our parents were so cracked out, Kris and I had to get out on these streets and do what we had to do to take care of home…I remember it like it was yesterday…

May 2000

It was the worst rainy day in Michigan. No one was supposed to be outside due to the severe weather, yet Kris and I was outside on the corner of the East side of Detroit. Not just any corner, we were on Mack Ave, also known as Murda' Mack. Many know of it, but have never been there due to their fear of getting murdered. But that didn't stop Kris and me from selling our dope. We stood in the pouring rain, in our matching red hoodies and sweatpants, ready to make more money.

"Babe it's getting late. You need to go home 'cause we got to go to school in the morning. And you know you've been fuckin' up in school lately."

Kris suggested. "I know." I responded in my baby voice. "You don't want them to find out what's going on and what we are doing on the low. I don't want them to take you away from me. You know you're my heart girl!" Kris said while staring into my green eyes. Every time he said that I'm his heart, I just wanted to melt.

"Ok baby..." I answered. Kris grabbed me by my hand and pulled me closer to him. He looked deep into my eyes, before placing a sweet kiss onto my lips. "Now hurry up girl." Kris said while smacking on my booty. "Whatever boy!" I laughed before heading home.

As I walked into my house with a smile on my face, eager to see Kris tomorrow, I heard voices coming from the kitchen. "This is what we are going to do Bubba Joe...We are going to bust into Big Man's house, take that money and some of that crack." The voice of my mom echoed. "But Tawny, you know Big Man will kill us if we did that." My father, Bubba Joe replied in his thick southern accent. "But baby, we need that crack." My mother pleaded. "Yeah," my father sighed. "We do...so when are we going to do this?" He asked.

While trying to sneak closer to the kitchen and be nosey, I accidentally stepped on my Siamese cat named Gina, causing her to scream in pain.

"What the fuck!" My mother yelled, looking into my direction. "Simone take yo' little ass to bed." She continued to yell sternly. "Ok." I sighed, putting my head down while I headed into my pitch black room. I laid in my cold bed and slowly drifted off to sleep. Hours passed when I was finally awakened by somebody grabbing my mouth, and dragging me out the room. I entered the illuminated kitchen only to see my father on his knees with a gun pointed to his

head by the infamous Big Man. Big man was 6'4',
340 pounds, with a vanilla wafer complexion due to
his Puerto Rican heritage. His jet black hair was
pulled back into a ponytail, and his honey colored
eyes was now cold and distant. "Please, please don't
kill me." My daddy pleaded. "Shut the fuck up!" Big
man yelled loudly.

<u>Kris</u>

I had a feeling that something was wrong when I
heard yelling coming from Simone's window. I
hopped out my bed, and peeked out my window only
to see my Uncle a.k.a Big Man, pointing a gun at Mr.
Simmons head. Next thing you know, Simone's mom
was pushing Simone towards Big man while saying,
"Here, take her! I know we took your money but her
pussy is worth more than that." "Mama!" Simone

cried in shock. "Shut up Simone." Mr. Simmons yelled, while still on his knees at gunpoint. "But I don't want to go sleep with him." Simone cried. "Shut the fuck up! You're going to lie down, you're going to take it, and you're going to like it damnit." Mrs. Simmons said firmly.

I couldn't believe my eyes, they were going to give my baby girl away and let my uncle take her virginity. I quickly grabbed my pistol from under my bed, placed it in my boxers, and made my way over to the house. I snuck in through Simone's bedroom window, which was always left open for me and crept closer to the hallway.

I stood and watched for a minute since her Siamese cat Gina was attacking Big Man's leg. "Fuck this stupid ass cat!" Big Man snarled. Grabbing the cat by the tail, Big Man threw Simone's cat in the air. With the cat high in the air over

Simone's head, Big Man shot the cat right in the stomach. Millions of pieces scattered all over the room and blood landed all over Simone. The look of shock and sadness hovered over Simone's face. From that alone, I couldn't take it.

I ran into the kitchen and started shooting. Big Man was first, and then I shot Mr. and Mrs. Simmons, for the foul shit that they tried to pull on my baby girl. Simone sat on the ground crying harder and harder each second. I couldn't stand to see my baby girl cry.

I ran over to her, pulled her into my arms, and allowed her to cry on my shoulder. All while I began to calmly speak to her. "Don't worry baby I'm going to take care of you, and I won't let anybody ever, ever, hurt you again. You know you're my heart girl." I meant every word I said, and I knew that it was my obligation to take care of her from now on.

2004

Four years has passed, and now Simone and I are living in our own house on the Westside of Detroit. The Hot Boyz affiliation was just starting to take off on these streets. All we had to do was take out the AK47 boys, and we would officially be the lead gang taking over Detroit. Hot Boyz becoming the new gang meant more territory, more work, and even better...More power. Smooth and I became cool ever since he moved up here from New York, and I met him through Samya. Smooth was different than the others out here trying to make a dollar. He was smart, and because of him, he introduced me to a new lifestyle.

This was the lifestyle of having others work under us as the movers and shakers, while we were the masterminds behind what we call a "business." This would be a sure fire plan, but first I had to take out the main crew of the AK47 boys. I had to kill them all by myself, and tonight would be the night. Simone and I sat in front of Saks bar and grill, waiting for them to come out so I can spray them down. I haven't done anything like this since I took out my Uncle and Simone's family four years ago. Sweat perspired down my forehead, while fear crept over me. I could see the six men coming out the bar. It was now time to do my job, but wait...What if they have a gun? What if one of them shoots back and killed us instead? What if?

So many thoughts clouded my mind, while I heard Simone's voice from the background. "Kris here they go!" She said. "Kris, get the gun!" "Kris...what the fuck are you doing?" Next thing I knew, Simone grabbed my Automatic Handgun and started spraying all six of them before my eyes. It all happened so fast, I just sat there in pure amazement. How could she do this and laugh about it?

"Did you see that shit?" She laughed. "I got that nigga right there in between his eyes. Brains were flying all over the place!" She exclaimed, in pure enjoyment. This chick was seriously crazy. "Girl, you're crazy…You know that?" I asked in shock, while we were speeding down the highway. She looked at me with a huge smile. "Ooo…I like that. That is going to be my new nickname. Crazy…But not with a 'C', Krazy with a 'K'… Since I'm apart of you Kris." She commented. Happiness gleamed all over her face while we drove home. From that day on, I knew that Simone was now going to be "Krazy" my new hit man.

Krazy:

After the day we took out the AK47 crew, Kris and I worked together when it came to his Hot Boyz business. I mean after all he did for me, I owed him my life. Whatever he would ask of me, I would do with no questions asked. I loved Kris with all my heart. He was my lover, my best friend, and more importantly he was my family. Without Kris, I had no one else, well that was before I met Sweetz at school. It was 2004, my freshman year in high school. I sat in the lunchroom by myself, since I trusted no one, male or female. That all changed when I spotted her. She was a small brown skin girl with her hair in cornrows, glasses that looked like mine, and was weeping low self-esteem. From what I seen, she looked like she had a lot of pent up frustration.

It was something about her that reminded me of myself. I had to get to know her, I felt like I had to take her into my life.

Making my way over to her, I sat next to her and greeted her with a simple "Hey". A simple hey became the start of a wonderful friendship that flourished on this beautiful day. Being around her made me feel like I was going to be able to have a normal life. To have a real friend that I had a strong connection with, a boyfriend who loves me, and to be able to go to school like a normal teenage girl, was truly a dream.

It was time to snap back to reality as I headed home from school, in my black caprice classic. I pulled up in front of my house only to see Kris sitting on the porch in a black hoodie that almost covered up his baggy pants, with the crispy black Air Force One sneakers. Whenever he was dressed in black, I knew it was time to make a move. We had a job to do, so there was no time to play.

I sat there in the car as he walked towards me, flashing me that sexy grin, and hopped into the passenger side. "What's good?" Kris greeted, while looking me up and down. I wanted to jump his bones right then and there, but I had to keep my composure, since we had business to handle. "Nothin'... So what's up?" I asked while staring into his eyes. The serious expression swept over Kris's face before he spoke. "I found out some info on that pussy ass nigga Quick. He is the leader of the AK47 boyz, and is the only thing that is preventing us from making that real money."

"Man, what I would do to kill that motherfucka' "I spat. "Don't worry mami you're going to have your chance to get this little bitch tonight!" Kris replied, causing a smile to creep over my face. "Good...I've been waiting on this shit." I said in excitement. "Yep. Now go cruise down to the Westside." Kris commanded, as he chilled back in his seat. Without another question asked, I pulled off and headed to the Westside.

The whole ride was silent until he told me to ride down Trinity Street. I slowly rolled down the street, until I spotted a whole bunch of guys chillin' at this one house. Kris quickly began to point out one of them to me. "You see that high yella' motherfucka' with the fitted on?" "Yeah." I answered, while taking a glance at the guy. "That's Quick. Your assignment tonight is to fuck him, get info, kill him, and leave no evidence." Kris explained coldly. "Okay." I replied, while turning down another street that led me down onto the highway. Within ten minutes we were back at our house, plotting on how to take this bitch out.

"I want you to go and get sexy for this party tonight where you will have to go and do your work." Kris explained as we headed upstairs into our bedroom. *"Ok baby."* I agreed. *"Now you're going to have to fuck him, but I don't want you let your emotions get into this shit ok?"* He asked while staring straight into my eyes, yet it felt like he was staring straight into my soul. I nodded my head in a trance, causing him to laugh his cute baby laugh.

"And one more thing..." Kris stated. *"What?"* I asked, finally getting impatient of standing. Kris continued to stand there, looking me over seductively before walking up and aggressively sucking all over my neck. I moaned lowly as I felt his hard dick pressing into my pussy. He started to suck on my ear while whispering *"I got to get you loose for the business you're about to be doin' ok?"* I nodded my head yes, as he ripped my sweats off, picked me up, and pent me up against the wall.

He held me with one hand, and with the other he pulled down his basketball shorts. With one quick thrust, he popped my cherry. This was my first time having sex, since I was still a virgin. Tears started to flow from my eyes as he pumped in and out of me furiously. I started to finally moan as he went deeper and deeper into my pussy. He gripped my hair, and continued to pump faster and faster as my juices started running down my legs.

I dug my nails into his back as he started to hit my g-spot, causing me to scream his name as I felt a warm sensation come over me and my body began to shake. I never felt like this before. More of my sweet juices flowed down my legs, as he passionately kissed me, and let me down. "Damn that shit was too good baby." Kris sighed, while rubbing his dick as he walked back into the bedroom. "Hell yeah." I laughed while following him.

"We are going to have to do that more often!" I joked. "Of course baby, now let's go take a shower." Kris replied, before walking up to me and kissing me passionately. Slipping his tongue into my mouth, he started gripping on my ass, causing my pussy to instantly get wet again. I would love to have a round two, but there was business that needed to be handled. I ended the kiss, grabbed his hand, and led him into the bathroom.

After our shower, I oiled up with my edible cherry flavored body oil, and slipped into my dress... with no underwear! This wasn't any old dress; this was a tight black strapless dress that stopped at my mid-thigh. When I say tight, I mean it was so tight that you could see my curves from a block away. It felt like my ass was about to fall out the bottom of my dress! I quickly walked into my room and started to put on my open toed stiletto heels that laced around my calves. After I finished lacing it up, I took a piece of ribbon and tied it around my thigh, to prevent exposure, and slid my blade under the ribbon. I grabbed my car keys and gave Kris a peck on the lips goodbye.

Unfortunately, before I could even walk out the front door, Kris threatened me by saying, "Look you said you were down and all, but if I find out that you ain't do what you had to do, I'm goin' to leave yo' ass toothless!" With that in mind, I hopped into my car and soon enough I was back on the Westside.

Anxiety crept over me when I pulled up to the house. I swear I was about to piss on myself! There was nothing but nigga's there, and I swear I was the only female there with the exception of the few hoes. I slowly parked around the corner and strutted back to the party. I walked up in there with all eyes on me, but that wasn't stopping me from completing my mission. I looked around for my victim, but he was *nowhere to be found in the living room area. I walked into the kitchen to get a drink when he walked in stumbling. Good, he was drunk!*

I observed every detail of him. He was wearing black Dickies pants, a white tall tee, with his left sleeve rolled up to show his tattoo that had a picture of a sad clown and a happy clown with words that said "Laugh now Cry later." His fitted hat was tilted to the left side and a toothpick hung out the corner of his mouth.

I gazed at him as he flowed through the kitchen and straight to the dance floor. I quickly grabbed my drink, and walked into the living room where everyone was freaking the hell out each other. I slowly switched my hips over to the couch where he was sitting, and I stood right in front of him. To appeal to him, I began to rub my thigh up and down slowly, yet seductively. "What's good with ya' mama?" Quick asked while licking his pink lips. "Shit, I was wondering the same thing about you." I replied in a sexy voice. "Shit chillin', you know what I mean." Quick smiled. Just then Play-N-Skillz song "Freaks" came on. "Do you dance ma'?" Quick asked, staring into my green eyes.

"Yeah but the question is do you?" I replied while licking my lips. "How about you find out?" He smiled. I lead my way to the dance floor, as he followed my ass like clockwork. I slowly started to grind my hips to the beat as he licked his lips.

Finally getting tired of standing there and watching' my ass move so seductively, Quick gripped me by waist pulling me closer to him, and started to dance with me. I looked deep into his eyes as I turned around, bent over to the front, and touched my toes. The harder I twerked him, the harder his dick got. As the song slowly faded, he *held my hand leading me back into the kitchen and started to pour me a drink. "Damn mama, you got a nigga on hard and shit." Quick commented with a smile, causing me to laugh. "What can I say I just got it like that, you know what I mean?" I said while seductively leaning on the counter. Quick looked at me up and down before responding. "Yeah, most girl's don't know how to work their shit right, like they're a virgin or something."*

I pulled him by his collar so that he could be in my face. "Well I am not like them hoes out there." I said, while nodding my head towards the living room. "I noticed that when you bent over and touched them toes... Making that ass clap for me." He smiled. Getting close to his ear, I began to whisper in a seductive tone. "Well if you like I can show you how that ass clap personally." "Aww shit I got me a freak!" Quick exaggerated. "Yeah, but first we got to play a game." I continued. "Aight then." He agreed, blindly entering the dangerous trap that I've set up for him.

Introducing Quick:

I stood there and looked at ole' girl as she grabbed the whole 5th of gin and grabbed my hand. I followed her all the way into the back room, and sat on the couch as she shut the door and astraddled my lap. "Okay this game is called 'You wish you can touch'." She started, while lightly grinding on my stiff dick. "Aight." I quickly replied.

"The rule is that whateva' I do to you, you can't touch me, and if you touch me, you have to tell me a top-secret thing about you." She explained. "Aight." I agreed. I sat back on the couch and looked at her as she stood up, downed some of the gin, and started to strip off her clothes.

I slowly slipped my hand into my pants and started to stroke my dick as she started to rotate her hips, and stripped until she was butt ass naked. She astraddle my lap once again, and started to grind on me while sucking on my neck. Pulling my hand out my pants, she replaced it with her hand, causing me to tilt my head back as her soft angelic hand stroked up and down my dick. She was stoking me so good, that my hands started to tremble! I wanted to grip her round, apple bottom ass so bad, but I couldn't. I almost nutted as she slid off my lap, pulled my dick out, and just popped it in her mouth like it was a lolli-pop.

My hands gripped the back of her head, forcing her to deep throat my dick, when all of a sudden she stopped with a wide grin on her face. She stood up in front of me, with that tempting body, and shook her index finger side to side.

"Nah uh baby boy, you can't touch, so you have to tell me something about yourself." She said while a smirk. "I'm part of the AK47 boyz." I said while gripping my dick and stroking it. "Okay I got me a thug huh?" She smiled. "Yep!" I smiled back, revealing my one dimple.

Krazy:

After he told me his one fact, I started to pour him drink after drink until that nigga was pissy drunk. His lips were too loose and he would not stop telling me all his information about the AK47 boyz. When I got all I needed to know out of him, I stood up ready to leave. Kris's voice popped into my head "Fuck them and kill them."

I sighed before leaning on the wall, planting one foot on the arm of his chair, and started to play with myself while looking deep into his eyes. I started to moan loudly when out of nowhere, he came up to me and rammed his hard dick into my throbbing wet *pussy. He gripped my waist as he plunged deeper and deeper.*

I grabbed a whole handful of his hair as he continued to pump in and out of me. His body began to shake rapidly, so I quickly pulled him out of my pussy, and started to suck his dick until he nutted down the back of my throat. That's when I quickly slipped out my blade, and cut him right by his dick and his ball sack. He screamed loudly, as he hit the floor holding his damaged privates.

I sat on top of him and held the blade under his Adams apple. "Nigga your fuckin' with the Hot Boyz." I said coldly. "Man, I don't know what you talking about." Quick cried. He started whining like a little baby, but I wasn't hearing it. "Well let me jog yo' memory." I replied with a smirk, before I slit his throat and poured the rest of the gin all over his body.

Taking the black lighter out his pocket, as well as a black and mild blunt, I lit the blunt, and took a puff. I looked over his body before rummaging around the room, searching for the items that I needed to finish him off. When I found what I was looking for, I took the box of matches that were out on the table, struck a match, and threw it on his lifeless body as I made my exit like nothing happened.

Feeling accomplished, I pulled up to my house and walked straight up to the room where Kris was.

"I did it." I said calmly. Kris choked on his spit. "You did?" He asked. "Yep. I lit him on fire!" I exclaimed. "Aww shit...You're on that hot boy shit!" Kris leaped up, getting all hype. "Hell yeah baby..." I started, but the thought of him threatening me earlier tonight hit me. "But I did it cause you threatened me..." I continued sadly.

"I only did it for you." Kris replied, while getting close to my face. "How the hell are you doing it for me?" I said while starting to cry. "That shit really hurt me baby." I finished. "I'm sorry baby, but I did that because of this..." Kris said while pulling out a suitcase filled with money.

"Is that mine baby?" I asked while wiping my eyes. "Yeah." Kris said with a smile. I jumped up and hugged him. "Thank you so much baby!" "I will do anything for you girl." Kris said, while holding me tighter in his arms. "I love you. You're my heart girl and you know that." Kris continued, looking into my eyes. "I love you too Kris..."was the last thing I said before walking into the bathroom to wash my body.

Standing under the shower head I recap the moments of tonight. Images of Quick's lifeless body pop in my head, even the smell of burnt flesh filled my nostrils. I slowly lowered myself into the bathtub *and held my knees close to my chest as tears rolled down my face. I could feel myself at my breaking point, I loved Kris and I loved the perks of this life but having this blood on my hands will haunt me for the rest of my life.*

CHAPTER 2: SHIT GETS REAL

3 months later

__Krazy__

I awoke to the sound of my alarm clock; I slowly rolled over and looked at the time only to see it was 11 A.M. Without hesitation, I hopped out of the bed and made my way into my private bathroom to get ready for the day. After taking a nice shower I got dressed as quickly as I could. I tossed on a pair of jeans and a plain black t-shirt and was ready to go. I had things to do and spending hours getting ready wasn't one. Grabbing my ponytail holder, car keys and my cell phone, I rushed down the stairs while tying my shoulder length hair up only to see Kris sitting on the couch.

"Hey baby you lookin' all fresh today" Kris's eyes gleamed from the sight of me. All I could do was smile in response. "Thank you baby," I said as I sat on his lap and gave him a quick kiss. "You know when you get back we got to handle some business today right?" Kris reminded me.

"Damn, that might have to wait" I said, thinking about all the things I had to do today. Yet, Kris was not having it. "What the fuck you mean it have to wait?" Kris snapped, as his voice got louder with anger. "I have to meet up with Sweetz today to go over a plan to take out this new crew and who knows how long that will take." I calmly spoke while giving him my pleading eyes "Well I don't know about you, but I'mma make this money so do what you fucking please." Kris said coldly, while pushing me off his lap.

I stood up and looked at him confused for a minute, but Kris ignored me as he suddenly stood up, grabbed his keys and headed out the front door without another word said. I walked up to the window and saw Kris hop in his all black crown Vic and pull off without looking back. I stood there looking out of the window not knowing what to do anymore. One minute we are a happy couple, then the next he treats me like shit. To me, joining this Hot Boyz crew was the worst idea we have ever done because our relationship has been going down the drain since then.

I heavily sighed as I grabbed my things and walked outside to my black caprice classic. I quickly pulled off listening to Waka Flocka Flames "Live by the Gun" as I made my way to Sweetz crib. I was so lost in my thoughts that the twenty-five minute drive took nothing but a couple of seconds. I pulled up in front of Sweetz crib only to see her sitting on the steps with that trick Cashmere!

Sweetz looked over to my direction and met my gaze and waved at me while giving me her priceless warm smile. I exited the car praying to God that Cashmere wouldn't stay long because as soon as she open her mouth to talk, you can't help but get irritated...

"Aye bitch, took you long enough! I called you last night what was going on?" Sweetz joking greeted. "Shit, you know how it is. Kris and I be making our moves." I replied nonchalantly. "Yea ya'll are the night creeping types...How is Kris by the way?" Cashmere said with a sneaky smile planted on her face. I sucked my teeth in response. "What the fuck does it matter how my man is doing?"

"Right!! Cashmere you be on that other shit asking about people men like you don't have one of your own!" Sweetz interjected with one raised eyebrow. "I just wanted to know since I ain't see him in a minute." Cashmere replied with a nonchalant manner, causing me to go off.

"And bitch if I ever hear his name slip out yo mouth again the last thing you will ever see is this barrel of my 9mm." I said as i pulled out my gun from my purse and aimed it in her face. Cashmere quickly put her hands up before speaking. "Damn Krazy I ain't mean no disrespect! I got a man and I ain't thinking about Kris."

I placed the barrel closer to her head, loving every minute of putting the fear into her. "You better not, EVER, in your life even think about what's mine! Or I'll take what's yours bitch!" Sweetz grabbed my arm, trying to stop me from taking this to another level. "Come on Krazy don't let her get to you...Just put the gun away so we can get down to business." She pleaded.

I stood there glaring at that dumb bitch! Everything about her just made me want to pull the trigger. I glared at her, looking like a pathetic excuse of women. Everything about her was fake, from her long Remy weave to her green contacts. From a quick glance at her, you could easily mistake her for me. At times, I think that this sad bitch wanted to be me. I clicked the safety lock on my 9mm and tucked it away safely in my purse. I gave Cashmere my prize winning smirk before walking into Sweetz's crib satisfied with scaring the living daylights outta that bitch.

I sat down in Sweetz's glamorous living room, where Liyah and Samya sat on the couch waiting. The petty shit was now over and we had real shit to handle.   For the next four hours, we sat there plotting on our next move to eliminate this new and upcoming crew. During this time my mind just wasn't there, all my thoughts ran back to what happened this morning between Kris and me. It seems that he has been more and more distant these past couple of months. The more we argue the hard it seems to focus on work. He sit up there and lecture about getting money but yet he the one causing me distraction!

I sat in the chair and nodded my head as Liyah explained what time we should execute the plan. But I kept thinking about all the signs that something was going terribly wrong in my relationship.... After everything was set up, I said my goodbyes and dipped off to the crib.

Sweetz

I circled around my bedroom lighting the candles when I was interrupted by a knock at my front door. I rushed to the front door only to reveal a tall dark silhouette; I smiled as he swooped me up into his arms carrying me into the bedroom, and laid me down gently onto the bed. We ripped each other's clothes off as we continued to kiss each other until we were almost breathless. I straddled his lap and slowly rode him up and down in a steady pace as he grabbed my hips. I looked down deep into his eyes, and swear this nigga got me hooked.

As I slowly rolled my hips he bit his lips cooing my name. *He* sat upright and kissed me so passionately that's when I decided to pick the pace up. I rode that dick up and down and round and round, causing his eyes to roll to the back of his head. I felt myself reaching my peak as I screamed his name. Both our bodies began to shake as we came together. He laid back onto the bed to catch his breath as sweat glistened on his sexy body. I took my place next to him, cuddling up under him real close. I kissed him on his neck and began to trail all the way up to his ear and whispered "I Love You Kris."

__Krazy__

I unlocked the door to the house after driving around the city doing my routine checks on the Hot Boyz trap houses making sure everything was straight for the night shift. I was so tired that I just dropped my purse and keys on the end table and made my way to the couch. I looked out the living room window and noticed that Kris car wasn't in the garage and that mothafucka left the garage door up... I sighed heavily in annoyance, just the thought that he came back and was in such a big rush to leave he left our garage open for the whole world can see what we had! I swear he knew nothing about keeping a low profile... Being exposed like this can either get your shit stolen or worse get you raided by the police! I pulled out my cell phone to call him but his phone went straight to voice mail. This shit is starting to get beyond irritating, first the petty arguments, then not answering his phone like he is avoiding me!

I can't help but wish that this shit would end, all I want is some peace of mind but dealing with this got my trigger finger itching. Day's and night's like this i just want to put him out his misery. I picked myself off the couch and walk into my room and turn on the TV. Letting my mind drift off until I fell fast asleep.

When I woke up the whole house was dark. I sat up and looked around to see if there was any signs of Kris but there was nothing just me in this big ass house alone. I rolled over and grabbed my cellphone off the night stand only to see I had no missed calls. I look at the clock on the phone and it read 4:00 a.m. on the dot...Now something ain't right, sitting here all day with not even a courtesy call to let me know if he alive isn't like Kris at all. I can't shake this feeling in my bones that something is going on.

I rolled off the bed and started to search through Kris closet when I came across his safe. I turned the dials and popped it open to reveal his gun laying there. I picked it up and open it seeing that all the bullets was in the clip. I held the gun close to my body as a single tear fell from my eye.

He never left the house without his gun and to see it here let me know that business was not what he was doing tonight or any other night he disappeared. How could he do this to me, my love, and that my family would do such an ultimate betrayal! We started from the bottom just to get here and all he has to show for it is disloyalty! I threw the gun back into the safe and walk out the closet and straight to the phone to call Sweetz. My hands was trembling so bad I could hardly dial her number. The phone rang once and went straight to voice mail. I sighed and hung the phone up. I just couldn't shake this feeling that something bad was brewing!

I laid back down and was twisting the promise ring Kris gave me around my finger deep in thought. I wanted to know who he is creeping with; I want to know her face. Because when I do I promise that I will be the last face that bitch will ever see! I grab Kris pillow and inhaled the scent of his cologne and slowly dozed off into a deep sleep.

<u>Kris</u>

I woke up later that afternoon in Sweetz bed in a daze, man that bitch knew how to work that pussy. Licking my lips I rolled out the bed and headed straight for the shower. I let the water run down my body as I replayed the scenes of last night in my head. I know Sweetz is my nigga girl and Krazy best friend but shit if a bad bitch throwing pussy yo' way who wouldn't hit it? I chuckled to myself as I got out the shower and started to get dressed, I walked back into the bedroom where Sweetz laid in the bed.

I walked up to her and ran my hands up and down her thigh as I kissed her lightly on the cheek. She stirred slightly in her sleep but still didn't wake up. Guess I put the dick down too good for her. I grabbed my keys and cell off the nightstand and made my way out her crib so I can meet up with Smooth at the spot to talk about hiring a free agent.

I sat in the office with Smooth while we talk about taking over the territory of the Street legends. Even though they gave use a piece of the territory we was looking to take over! Smooth gave me the name of the free agent that was well known for his work and told me to plug him in a quick as possible. I left the spot and headed home, pulled up to the crib like an hour later and notice Krazy car still parked in the driveway. Fuck ain't this bout a bitch! I was hoping that she would still have been out since she had to go to the different Hot Boys mansions to pay the staff since today was payday.

Hesitantly, I got out the car and pulled out the house keys. I unlock the door and peaked my head inside only to be greeted by a cold quiet house. It was way past 12 o'clock in the afternoon and Krazy not being home is really odd since her car was parked. She usually got up early to drop off the money to the housekeeping staff so for only her car being here had my mind wondering.

I pulled out my cell phone to see I had 13 missed calls from Krazy but they was all from last night. I slipped my phone back into my pocket as my heart started to race. Could it be that she caught on to Sweetz and I? But she couldn't have cause if she did me nor Sweetz would have been in the land of the living this morning. I closed my eyes and took a deep breath to calm my nerves before I dialed her number all for it to ring twice before she answered.

"Hello." Krazy said dryly over the phone. "Hey baby what's good with you?" I asked, playing it off. "I should be asking you that." She spat, "What you mean?" I asked innocently. "Don't play dumb with me Kris where the fuck was you last night to the wee hours of the morning?" Krazy answered with attitude. "Girl get that attitude out of yo' voice. Mann, I was just handling business." I added, causing Krazy to laugh. "So you're really about to play games right now like I'm stupid? What real nigga handle business without his burner? So let's try this again...Where, better yet who, was you doing last night?" She continued.

All I could do was laugh in response. "You think you so smart huh? You really think that I would do some dirty shit like that to you?" "I don't know what you would do anymore..."Krazy said coldly. "Damn Simone so you're going to sit on the phone and act like you don't know me? You're going to sit on this motherfucking phone and act like my words hold no loyalty!" I yelled.

"With everything that's been going down these past couple of months, no I don't!" Krazy replied, causing me to chuckle over the phone at her stupidity. "Well I advise you to get yo' mind right! And if you really want to know what I've been up to, then go ahead and hit Smooth up." I suggested before hanging up the phone in her face.

<u>Krazy</u>

I pulled the phone from my ear in disbelief that Kris had the audacity to hang up in my face. I sat on top of the picnic bench in front of the library dressed in my red sweat pants and my fitted black tee with my hair in a swoop side ponytail, just puffing a cigarette thinking of what I done months ago before Kris called. I went to go pay all the staff at the Hot Boyz mansion and talk to the head housekeeper Maria and slip her a couple hundred for her to keep her ears open about Kris comings and goings from all the mansions. I knew he had been creeping on me but I needed to know who and how many hoes he has been fucking with on the low.

My thoughts were interrupted by a deep male voice holding a conversation behind me. I turned around only to see a man standing there that was 6'4 with a cinnamon brown sugar skin complexion, he had the most exotic chocolate brown, almond shaped eyes I had ever seen! His dreads touched his collarbone and he had tattoos that covered his whole upper body that I could see through his wife beater. The tattoo that stood out the most was the tattoo around his collar bone that read "Gutta" in front of the Detroit Skyline.

I sat there in a daze until he look at me licking his luscious full lips before flashing me his pearly white Colgate smile. That's when I noticed the diamond filled grill on his bottom teeth. Just the sight of all the diamond and gold in his mouth sent my body into a frenzy. I quickly turned around, embarrassed for getting caught staring at him so hard. My face started to get hot as I felt his eye's roaming my body.

I stood up quickly to head home to prevent me from getting into a situation that I couldn't get myself out of! The last thing I needed in my life was to get curious about a nigga just because I'm going through some hard times with Kris, I said to myself when the thought came into my head. Why do I have to be the loyal one? I put just as much into this relationship and our partnership within the Hot Boyz. Because of that, I think it's about that time for me to get out of my character, but am I really ready to go against Kris? The man that saved me.

I started to make my way down the street when someone grabbed my arm. Out of instinct, I pulled my gun out of my purse and aimed it straight for a kill shot right in the middle of the person's forehead.

"Aye young thang ease yo' mind, I just wanted to know why you dipped off like that after I caught you staring at me..." The mysterious man said as his hands was up in the air to show that he didn't mean any harm. I was surprised at how calm he was considering that a gun was aimed at him. But I wasn't fooled; out here you can't trust any niggas, not even the one you're fucking. "Is that the only reason you followed me?" I asked with my gun still aimed for the kill shot.

"Yeah...or is that too suspicious for ya' Miss Gangsta?" He chuckled, like this was a mere joke to him. I immediately felt insulted. Did he think this was a fuckin game? "Don't you mock me like I won't pull the trigger." I spewed as I placed the gun up against his head. "No doubt you would, but in this situation I know you won't." He said confidently as he pulled out a black 'n' mild from his pocket and began lighting it, not even phased by the revolver on his forehead.

"How sure are you?" I asked, as I pulled the hammer back shifting the bullet into the chamber. He inhaled his smoke before he began. "100% sure...You ain't bout to pull the trigger until you find out my name." I don't know what was coming over me, usually I would have pulled the trigger on the spot, with no conversation at all, yet instead, a smile crept over my face.

"Is that right...So what is the name?" "See for yourself." He said as he pulled the collar of his shirt down. "So the names Gutta eh?" I said. "Yeah, so what's good, who you down with?" He interrogated. "The Hot Boyz...you?" I held the gun tighter just in case he may have been my enemy. "Myself." He simply answered. "So you a free agent?" I asked as I lowered my gun. "Yes. I work for my damn self." He continued. "So that's why you was so chilled." I said, as I concealed my weapon back into my purse.

"Any real hit man ain't scared to look death in its eye's." Gutta stated. "Is that right?" I chimed in, as I looked at him and noticed the smirk appear on his face. The fact that we both didn't fear death and could look it in the eye made me feel an instant connection. Yet I knew that a connection was not what I needed to develop with Kris still in my life. We continued to stare into each other's eyes, as the intensity and attraction increased. Never in my life have I felt something like this, but I knew that I had to cut it short as reality began to set in. Without another word said, I turned around and sashayed away, leaving him stand in front of the library in a daze.

Thoughts of Gutta filled my mind as I made my way home. I walk through the door only to see Kris sitting in the kitchen sipping a glass of Hennessy while talking on the phone. I sat down at the table while he finished his conversation.

"Fasho my nigga we gonna have to link up tonight so we can get this plan concrete and you can meet up with my other hit man...I already know how you cut. I know you like to be on the solo tip but I feel like we need as much man power as possible so we can take ova you feel me? But nigga we can chop it up tonight... aight fasho." Kris concluded before hanging up.

"Wassup?" Kris greeted, giving me his full attention. "Nothing so what's going down?" I said mildly irritated from our conversation earlier. "Smooth and I want to take over the whole Street Legend's territory, so I linked up with a free agent that could get me more info on these nigga's. If he talking a good price I might even hire him as a partner." He explained. "What the fuck? We don't need outsiders involved in our affairs." I snapped, causing Kris to get loud in defense "That ain't your call to make! If I say we need more manpower than that's what the fuck is going to go down."

"Are you fucking serious, last time I checked we were a team Kris! You going to Smooth making moves without telling me is a whole new type of low! Even for you!" I yelled. "Simone let's get this straight whenever Smooth ask for my opinion it doesn't involve you. Don't forget your place in this crew." Kris snapped back. "My place! What place is that Kris?" I egged on. "Doing what the fuck I tell you to do!" Kris yelled in anger.

I sat there looking Kris right in his eye's with the coldest look I could give him. Nothing else needed to be said, because this nigga has lost his mind. It's amazing what a little power can do to a person. I stood to exit the room when Kris came up from behind me, wrapping his arms around my waist, and nuzzling his face into my neck.

"I know that was harsh, but baby this dude might open a lot door for us, plus I'm going to be leaving town for a while." Kris said apologetically. "What?" I yelled out in shock from his new announcement. "Smooth and I and a couple others are heading to Atlanta to expand the empire." He explained calmly. "But Why Atlanta?" I posed. "I'm not sure why, but while I'm gone you'll need to hold things down for the Hot Boyz." Kris answered.

I sighed heavily before letting out an "I understand..." "Plus this free agent is getting paid extra to stay by yo' side. I can't have you out here on the solo tip you feel me?" Kris explained. "I can handle my own!" I said full of attitude. "I know you can, but this is more for me then you. You my heart Simone." Kris reassured his love for me.

<u>Kris</u>

Right then and there I knew I had Krazy right back where I wanted her. I knew my baby couldn't stay mad at me for too long. I started to kiss and suck on her neck just to tease her, causing her to let out that low, soft moan that got my dick on hard. I pulled her shirt off and started to caress her breast. I nibbled on her neck down to her collar bone while pulling her sweat pants down when out of nowhere my phone started to ring. I quickly answered my phone only to hear the voice of the free agent saying he was pulling up.

"Sorry baby we are going have to finish this later." I said as I kissed her on her cheek. "Yeah, ok." Krazy shrugged while putting her clothes back on. I knew she was sexually frustrated but she would just have to wait. Business always came first. I quickly ran upstairs to the bathroom to run some cold water over my face and help calm myself down, when the doorbell rang. I yelled down the stairs to Krazy telling her to get the door…

Krazy

After adjusting myself I walked out of the kitchen towards the front door. When I opened the door I saw this tall silhouette, so I clicked on the porch light only to see Gutta standing there with the glistening smile of his. All I could think was damn! What am I about to get into?

"What's good with ya young thang?" He smiled, leaving me in pure shock. "So you the one the Hot Boyz hired…""Is that a problem for you?" He laughed lowly.

"It's not my place to have a problem with their decisions" I said, before letting him into the house.

"And I'm taking it you're the partner I'm going to be working with for the next couple of months?" Gutta asked as he eyes traveled up and down my body. I sat on the couch and slowly crossed my legs, just too lightly tease him. "Yes that would be me." Gutta licked his lips before speaking, "Why a pretty thang like you out here getting blood on your hands?"

Before I could answer, Kris walked into the room with us, ready to start the meeting. "Aight so what's the information that you have to give me on the Street Legends?" Kris jumped in. "Well there is three waves of these nigga's. The highest in command are the Ole G's. They are the hardest to get to, but then there's the second in command and the third in command, if you trying to take over the whole territory your best bet is to wipe out the lower ranks first." Gutta explained.

<u>Kris</u>

Gutta continued to tell me about the Street Legends and how he and Krazy would kill off their men one by one. The plan was all coming together when my phone started to ring. I looked down and noticed that it was Sweetz calling me, so I instantly pushed her to voice mail. Not even a second later she called again! What the fuck could be going on?

"Hold on y'all I gotta take this phone call. This is some business shit." I said before exiting the room. Krazy eyed me suspiciously as I walked outside and answered the phone only to hear what seem like Sweetz crying in the background.

"What's wrong?" I asked with annoyance. "I need you here." She demanded. "What the fuck you mean you need me there? Do you understand what type of position you put me in when you call me! You're acting like Krazy won't hesitate to kill you or me!" I snapped. "At this moment I don't give a fuck what Krazy is going to do to me...I need you to come over right now!" She yelled over the phone, causing my blood to boil. "Bitch do you understand that's not a mothafuckin' option right now. I got business to handle a Kra...." I started but was quickly cut off by Sweetz "I'm pregnant!"

As soon as those words came out of her mouth, my heart just dropped. Pregnant? She can't be...this had to be a mistake! After telling Sweetz I was about to leave and be on my way, I walked back into house only to see Krazy and Gutta mapping out the targets. Krazy looked up at me and met my gaze. Looking deep into her green eyes I knew I had to make this right. Sweetz could not have this baby because if she does, Krazy will lose the only sanity she has left.

"I got an emergency phone call so I gotta be out." I interrupted. "Why?" she asked full of skepticism. "I can't explain all that you right now! I be back..." I said annoyed, before I walked outside and headed to my car.

Krazy

I watched Kris as he rushed out the door and hop in his car. I sat there staring at the plan we mapped out, as Gutta words went in one ear and out the other. For Kris to run out like that just answered my questions and all my doubts that it's someone else. There was so many holes in his story that it doesn't make any sense.

I tried to shrug off the feeling that something wasn't right as I turned around to finish the game plan but my mind drifted off and the next thing I knew, my focus was on Gutta's chocolate brown eyes. I couldn't help but stare, as my eyes traveled down to his full lips. My body was telling me to let out the pent up frustration while my mind was telling me no. When all of a sudden Gutta's voice ranged in my ear.

"Aye young thang you hear me or are you just going to stare at me with that cold blank look all night?" He asked, causing me to snap out of my trance. "Yeah, I heard you just fine nigga! I was just thinking about the plan." I said with an attitude. "Well young thang, you know you never answered my question." He smirked. "And what question was that?" I asked as I sat back onto the couch crossed my legs.

"How someone as pretty as u getting blood on your hands?" Gutta said, as he looked deep into my eyes. I felt uneasy by his intensity. "Umm, I'm not sure what u mean? What you think I ain't capable of doing the job or something?" I said, becoming defensive. Gutta began to scoot closer to me on the couch. "Not at all, "He began as he gently grabbed my hand. "Just your hands are so soft but yet stained with blood, then your features are not of a killer." He continued.

I gazed so deep into his eyes as chills came up my legs an in between my thighs. No one had ever said anything like that to me, not even Kris. I bit my bottom lip as I tried to scoot away from him but he pulled me closer into his muscular chest as he leaned close to my ear and whispered, " Someone like you needs to know what genuine loves feel like, being this hard core hit man seems all like a front to me. When the sweet reality of it is you forgot how it felt to be a woman, to be touched like a woman, treated like a woman and I just want to give you that moment. Can I do that for you?"

I looked up into his eyes as he massaged my lower back. I looked away from his intense gaze because I knew in the back of my mind that I wanted him bad, but then again, I was still with Kris and I couldn't do this to him, but my body was betraying me. My thoughts were racing when I felt his soft velvet hand caress my face. His strong hand forced me to look back into his intense gaze; my lips trembled as I gave into my body's betrayal and passionately kissed him. He slowly intertwined his tongue with mine, as he laid me back on the couch. We both gasped for air, as the sexual tension increased till it was so thick in the room.

As he caressed my body, I ran my fingers through his dreads and he began to give me butterfly kisses all over my neck. He undressed me slowly as I rubbed on his firm abs. Excitement surged through my body as I could feel his manhood growing in-between my legs. We finally managed to rip each other's clothes off before he gently entered me and began stroking in a steady pace. The whole time he looked me in my eyes, like he was looking through my soul. This was something that I never experienced before.

That night I shared the most passionate sex with Gutta, we shared a connection so deep that I was speechless.

As soon as we were finished, I quickly gathered my clothes and I walked into the bathroom to freshen up, I looked at my disheveled hair and the red marks all over my neck and collarbone rubbed my hand over them knowing the hickeys would soon appear. All I could think about was how guilty I felt yet how good my body felt at the same time. I splashed some water over my face and fixed my hair before exiting out the bathroom, and heading back to the living room, walking back to living room only to see Gutta standing by the window putting his shirt back on. He turned around and looked me straight in the eyes and flashed me that priceless smile that gave me shivers up and down my spine.

"You alright young thang?" He asked. "Yeah, I'm good." I said calmly, as I sat back down on the couch. "Yeah, alight...well tomorrow we got to do a stake out of the first wave of the Street Legends. So rest up tonight." Gutta reminded me, as he gathered the rest of his things. "Oh ok, just swing through tomorrow." I suggested as I walked him to front door. "Aiight young thang, you be smooth." Gutta replied before kissing me on the forehead, and making his exit.

I leaned up against the closed door and let out a long sigh. "What the fuck am I doing?" was all I could ask myself. Everything felt so right but was dead wrong! Kris would never forgive me for this, but deep down inside I didn't care. He's been fucking around on me, and it's not like I planned to do this. I just couldn't deny the connection I had with Gutta was so strong that it was suffocating!

As expected, Kris didn't come home the next morning, so the day went on as usual. I went to different trap houses and checked out stats, and then I met up with Liyah to collect debts owed to the Hot Boyz. By the time I made it back to the house, I was so tired and my hands were bruised from beating the man that owed the Hot Boyz money. This line of work was taking its toll on my body, my mind, and my soul. Just as I went to lay across my bed, my phone began to ring. It was the one and only Gutta, reminding me that the plan was that to link up around midnight and that he would come and scoop me up.

It finally struck midnight and it was time to do the first stakeout with Gutta. We both rocked all black from our hoodies with the dickie pants, to our black skull hats and our timberland boots. We sat in his all black marauder, with the presidential black tinted windows, across the street from the main trap house of the Street Legends. Anticipation crept over us as we waited for their arrival. Within five minutes, a candy painted red Lexus SUV rolled up in front of the house. We watched as a short and thick, Asian female with bright red hair hopped out the car.

"You see that girl right there?" Gutta asked as he was smoking a black and mild. "Yeah..." I nodded. "That's Red, she's the head female of the third in command. She basically controls all the prostitution rings in the 'D. She set up shop in all the strip clubs on Michigan Ave. She also does a little stripping on the side to keep a low profile since she is well known out here on these streets. She got a house out on the eastside, where her hired lookalike name Ciara lives, just to throw off anyone who is looking for her. But she actuality she lives in Ann Arbor..."As Gutta continued to give me the lowdown on Red, A black Hummer truck pulled up behind Red's car.

Two men jumped outta the expensive truck dressed in white long sleeved thermals under black tall tees, Cartier glasses, true religion jeans, and some black timbs. This was typical Detroit hood nigga status. One was brown skinned with a baby face and had a slicked back ponytail; while the other one was dark skinned with a low fade. They both wore flashy blinged out chains that I could see a mile away. I shook my head and laughed at the sight of them. Why would a gangsta be so flashy when they know that there is many possibilities that enemies are always watching them? If anything, they need to be low key and live discreet lives.

"I know you see those wack ass niggas out there. The one with the ponytail is named Slick. He is known to be a slick mothafucka' with the ladies and can persuade the hell out of some niggas in a business deal. While the other one with the flashy chains is 40 Cal. He is the one who does the hits and be robbing niggas. Both of them are always at the Shadow bar on Fridays and at the Kingdom club on Saturdays. After the club you can catch them at the strip club on Fridays and at the MGM on Saturdays." Gutta explained. "They make themselves easy to find with their dumb asses." I chuckled. "Hell yeah!" Gutta laughed. "But that's good for us!" He continued. "Yeah less work..." I agreed.

We sat there for hours watching their workers clock in and out, as the three heads of command stayed in the house guarded by two men, one at the front door and one at the back door. You can tell that they was new to the game how they had high traffic coming from the house, and like typical nigga's having their little hoes stop by. All you seen was females running around in nice ass cars! They was just throwing them money like it wasn't shit. We was parked there all night and not even once did anyone notice us. Around five that morning they left out leaving their henchman to handle the light work, so that was our queue to make our way back to our side of town.

We pulled up in front of my house where Kris stood on the porch on his cell. I sighed as I turned to Gutta who just looked at me pleasantly, as if Kris wasn't even there. "Aiight young thang, you be smooth. I'mma hit you up a 'lil later." He stated. "Aiight then." I concluded.

Before I was able to slip out the car, Gutta grabbed my bruise filled hand eyeing me sympathetically. I pulled my hand away ashamed that he had to witness me being in such a bad state slipped out the car without even looking back and started to walk slowly towards the porch as Gutta pulled off. I stood on the porch waiting for Kris to say something but he just got off the phone and stood there real quiet. I stood there wanting him to say something, I wanted an explanation, or even an argument... just some type of reaction out of him! But there was nothing just him looking off into the early morning sky deep in thought like something was bothering him.

I stood there a moment before walking into the house heading straight into the bedroom, stripping off all my clothes and slipped into bed. I rolled over thinking about the information Gutta and I collected today when the bedroom door creaked open and

Kris stepped into the room. I heard him taking off his clothes before slipping in the bed behind me and wrapped his arms around my waist and kissed me on my neck before whispering in my ear.

"You sleep baby?" He asked. "No, what's up?" I asked as I rolled over. "You know I love you right?" Kris started as he began rubbing my face "Yeah, what's wrong?" I said full of concern. Kris let out a deep sigh before responding. "I fucked up, man I fucked up real bad." "Whatchu' mean you fucked up? What did you do?" I asked urgently, as I sat up in my bed.

Kris met my gaze as he sat up and kissed me passionately on the lips. I fell back onto the bed, as he laid on top of me kissing me from my ear to my neck; whispering how he was so sorry over and over again, and with one quick thrust he entered me. He thrusted in and out of me at a fast pace as I moaned and sucked on his neck. I screamed out his name as he brought me deep pleasure.

"I want you to have my baby." He whispered in my ear. "Kris don't play with me." I looked back at him, yet was taken aback by pleasure as he thrusted deeper inside me. "Say u want my baby!" Kris demanded. "Yes Kris, I want yo baby! Please let me have yo baby" I cried out in between my moans.

We both climaxed together as he collapsed still inside me kissing me while telling me how much he loved me. I wrapped my arms around him as we laid there in each other's sweat, sharing the same air 'til we both fell into a deep sleep with the sunlight peeking through our window. Yet my peaceful sleep was ruined by my mind wandering. I kept replaying the moment when Kris said he fucked up, and I couldn't help but feel like this thing he did would come back and bite me one day. I was his heart and even though we just made love I couldn't bring myself to forgive him. Any man who just did something wrong will act right for a while, but a tiger never changes his stripes.

~~~

The next couple of days Kris and I seemed to be getting along like the good old days, there was no more arguments and Kris always made sure that he was home when I got back from business with Gutta or anything affiliated with the Hot Boyz. Even though I was happy that things was getting back to normal, the damage has already been done and I started to question my feelings for Kris. At times I felt like the only reason why we were still together was because our history.

Flashback:

I was only in the sixth grade when I had my first encounter with ratchet bitches. There I was minding my own business trying to get off the city bus and walk home from school, when all of them surrounded me.

"Where you think you going you dirty gutter rat?" The main girl Mia yelled out. She was a tall and thick light skinned girl with hazel eyes and sandy hair styled in the swoop weaved ponytails. Mia was known as the popular eighth grader in school who always rocked the spray painted white tees, with the matching spray painted timberland boots, and the name plated belt buckle.

"Excuse me?" My eyebrow raised up in confusion.

"You heard me you black ass monkey! I don't even see why you come to school." She laughed.

"Your crack head parents can't even afford to buy your dirty ass new clothes." She continued.

"Yeah and you smell! Have your parents even heard of soap! Then you even have Kris fine ass following yo' stank ass around! You make him look bad! Everyone knows he should be with Mia!" Mia's friend Duchess added in.

"What makes ya'll think I make him do anything?" I yelled out in defense, only to be slapped with intensity by Mia. I fell back onto the ground holding my face in shock as Mia yelled "Shut your black ass up! Stay away from Kris bitch!"

Before I knew it Mia and her friends jumped me. I laid there on the ground in the fetal position as they stomped me and pulled my hair. I laid there on the dirty ground as they continued to whoop my ass. As they started to walk away, I sat up and dusted myself off as much as I could before walking home. I sat on my porch steps with my salty tears streaming down my face, causing the cuts and bruises all over my face to burn. I swear I hate school! Every day in that place felt like being in the pits of hell, besides Kris I had no friends and to make matter worse, we wasn't even in the same classes.

All of Kris classes was on the other side of the school. Day in and day out I was tortured by all the bitches in my class, since I wasn't considered pretty due to my dark skin. All the teachers looked at me with pity as all the kids in my class treated me as the outcast. Every day I had to talk myself out of committing suicide because I knew that my life wasn't like an average middle school girl. All of these thought swirled around in my head, as I looked down at my worn out air force ones that should be white but now are faded dirty beige. While all the girls in school were wearing the latest fashion of Rocawear and Babyphat, all I had to my name was dollar store tee shirts and thrift store pants.

My fucked up thoughts were abruptly interrupted when I heard the fence creak open, quickly wiping my face I looked up only to meet eye to eye with Kris's piercing grey eyes.

"Aye Simo....WHAT THE FUCK HAPPENED TO YOUR FACE?" Kris yelled. "It's nothing just got into it with some girls from school...it's nothing to be worried about." I said, laughing it off. The last thing I wanted was for Kris to worry because he always is going around taking my issues as his own.

"Who did this to you?" He asked sternly. "It was just Mia and them...you know how that shit be I shouldn't have let my guard down." I answered as I put my head down in shame.

I couldn't even look at Kris; I was so ashamed that I constantly have him worried about me even though we both was living a hard life. I started to grind my teeth out of frustration cause that bitch Mia and her friends caught me off guard at the bus stop and made a fool out of me.

"Fuck that shit we about to handle this today!" He spat as he grabbed my arm. I quickly pulled my arm back in objection. "Wait Kris I don't want any more trouble! Foreal just forget about it!"

He let go of my arm and looked into my eyes. "How do you expect me to let anything go when they did something like this to your face? I can't forgive them for what they did to you! You're so much more than that Simone, why you think I'm fucking with you and not them? Now we goin' over there and we ain't leavin' 'til you beat every last one of those hoes!"

Tears filled my eyes as Kris led me down the street to Mia's house. As always all those bitches was just chilling on her porch. I was so terrified that my hands started to shake, but Kris just held my hand tighter before smiling at me then he addressed Mia in a way that I will never forget.

"Aye yo Mia, you and yo boards put they hands on my girl?" "Naw Kris there's been a misunderstanding" She answered nervously. "Oh really understand this, all that shit you be talking about Simone is going to end today!" Kris said full of anger.

After that, Kris pushed me towards them and stood back with his arms crossed. I looked at him and back at Mia before walking towards her and the group of girls. I was so scared that I felt like I was going to piss on myself. But what they did to me was unforgivable and I couldn't let Kris look bad for picking a girl like me. All the rage and anger built up inside of me as I started to whoop on Mia and her friend's ass one by one. I was on they ass like a pit-bull in a dogfight.

From that day on no bitch in their right mind stepped to me. They all looked at me in respect, and little by little my looks started to change from a filthy poor black chick to a thug chick, no more dollar store tee shirts and busted shoes. I started rocking nothing but the best thanks to Kris. He made sure I had everything I needed and more. Kris became more then my boyfriend he became family......

As we currently rode back towards the house my mind shifted with thoughts of Gutta. During the following nights, I was out with Gutta planning out moves, and I felt like I was actually starting to get to know him... the real him. It was something in me that just yearned for him, but I couldn't let that feeling get the best of me.

Everything about Gutta was totally different from Kris. I was able to let my hair down around him, and I felt like I was more than a member of the Hot Boyz crew, I wasn't just the chick that got called to put people in their place and to knock them off. The connection I had with Gutta was beginning to grow, yet at the end of the day we still had to handle business.

The day of our first hit came by so fast I couldn't believe it. I wasn't nervous, but my adrenaline was pumping rapidly. I was ready for this moment. I've been playing the scene over and over again in my head since Gutta pitched the idea to me. I stood in the bathroom getting dressed to meet Gutta at the Shadow Bar. I slipped into my violet colored corset with some black shorts and finished it off with my peep toe purple heels. I went to the hair shop earlier that day so my hair was looking fly as shit. My bang was swooped to perfection as my high ponytail came to the mid of my back. I was putting on the finishing touches to my makeup when Kris walked in the bathroom, wrapping his arms around me and kissing me on my shoulder blade.

"You looking sexy baby." He said, as he stared at me through the mirror. "Thank you" I smiled. "Aight well, I'm about to head out and handle some shit, but I'm going make sure I finish in time to be home when you get back." Kris reassured me. "Okay that sounds good." I replied. Kris smiled and playfully slapped my ass and said, "You make sure you a good girl aight" before walking out.

I smiled as Kris exited the room; I turned and looked at myself in the mirror getting my game face on. I walked outside and hopped in one of my favorite trucks, my all black range rover. A couple of minutes later, I pulled up in front of the club and stepped out making sure that I flaunted my curves as I walked into the club.

I walked straight to the bar, and stood there for a couple of seconds when someone wrapped their arms around my waist. Quickly turning around, I was only greeted with a smile filled with diamonds. I smiled as I looked up at Gutta in his all black attire while his dreads was pulled back into a neat ponytail.

"Don't you look tasty" He licked his lips. I smiled and laughed in response.

"Well thank you, but you blowing my cover!" "Naw you already know I wouldn't have approached you if it would jeopardize our plan. Everyone is in V.I.P "Gutta explained. " Ok so why are you here then?" I asked. "I have something for you" Gutta hinted. "What is that?" I said as I leaned against the bar. "This…" Gutta said as he handed me something.

I looked down at the V.I.P pass he gave me, I swear this dude have connections with everybody. I gave Gutta a quick kiss on the cheek before I made my way up to the V.I.P section where I spotted the targets. Slick was sitting on the couch next to 40 cal and I must say they was dressed to impress in their all white Polo shirts with matching fitted caps, and the crispy black True Religion jeans! Their ice around their Cartier Frames glistened just as much as their neck and wrist piece. I walked straight up to them with so much confidence and took a seat next to them while playing my role.

"So is anyone going to offer me a drink?" I said out loud. Slick was the first one to respond. "Oh my bad shawty, what you drinking on tonight?"

"Nothing but the best!" I gleamed. "Of course" Slick licked his lips as his eyes roamed all over my flawless body. "So which one of you are going to get my drink?" I asked as I seductively crossed my legs. "Here you go lil mama" said 40 Cal, as he handed me my glass of Dom Perignon. "Thank you sweetheart." I smiled before sipping on my drink.

I sat there having a long conversation with the both of them, but my main focus was on Slick. I knew if I got him interested in me, then I would have him in the palm of my hand. Once I got Slick, then I knew that 40 would follow. I led Slick out to the dance floor, after a few more drinks, and I must say I twerked the mess out of him! I had him sucking all over my neck, while gripping my hips like he was going to fuck me right then and there on the dance floor. I knew I had him when the club closed and he followed me to my car like a little puppy.

"So why don't you swing by my place?" Slick suggested as he opened my car door for me. "Mmm, I don't know about that even tho' there's a whole lot of things I would love to do to you." I said flirtatiously. "Fasho my baby, I respect that! if it's more comfortable for you, one of yo' friends can come by my crib wit' you." Slick said, rubbing his hands together as his eyes roamed up and down my body.

"Oh no I don't like to share." I said while pulling him by his collar and began to whisper in his ear, "How about you and yo' friend come by my place so I can show you both a good time. I would love to let y'all both see how this pussy feel."

Slick licked his lips in response and smiled. "That what it is then! Let me get that address and I I'mma be there shortly. I wanna give you some time to prepare for this dick I'm 'bout to lay on you." I kissed his cheek in response. "Don't keep me waiting." I said as handed him the piece of paper with the address.

He shut my car door and I swiftly pulled off. I zoomed down the street I instantly called Gutta and told him to get ready since our guest would be there soon. I pulled up the abandon warehouse and parked my car in the front. Gutta stood outside the sliding doors dressed up as a butler. I winked at him as I walked inside, only to see that he had the warehouse fixed up as plan. I walked into the back room to change into my outfit and waited for Gutta to give me my queue.

Gutta

I stood outside when Slick and 40 Cal pulled up in an all-white charger. They looked a little on edge so I made sure to keep my role as believable as possible. I walked up to their car when 40 Cal rolled down the window.

"This way sir, Ms. Qiyana is expecting you." I said in a British accent.

Slick

I looked at 40 giving him a head nod letting him know everything was cool. We got out the car and followed the butler into the warehouse. At first I was skeptical about this whole situation, but when we entered the building I was in awe! This bitch must be a big time roller. The front entrance area was furnished in red oak wood floors beneath the gold dangling chandeliers lit with candles. The furniture was top of the line with an all-white chaise lounge chair, and two white chairs in front of the lounge chair. Me and 40 sat in the chairs as Qiyana walked into the room wearing a leather cat suit that showed off all her curves. And she had the thigh high black leather boots to match! Man this bitch was that shit!

She walked in with confidence, swaying her hips side to side as she walked to the lounge chair and laid across it like she was a queen. My dick was rising as she stared deep into my eyes while giving me a lustful grin.

"So do you guys like what you see?" She asked. "Shit like is an understatement..." I said as I was getting ready to stand up. She quickly stopped me by waving her finger side to side. "No no no young man, you can have a seat and mama will come to you." She said. "Ok mama" I smiled and sat back down. "So do y'all like to play games or like to get straight to the point?" She asked as she stood up, showing off those sexy curves once again.

"We like games" 40 and I both said. "A little foreplay wouldn't hurt nobody." 40 Cal gleamed in excitement. "Great!" She said before she snapped her fingers.

When she snapped her fingers, her butler came out with a gold tray with blindfolds on them and handed it to us. I picked up the blindfold and looked at her in confusion, but she just smiled and licked her lips seductively. "It's all a part of the game just relax." She reassured.

Gutta

I stood there in the corner of the room and watched Krazy as she walked up to Slick and astraddled his lap and slid his blindfold over his eyes. She started to suck on his collar bone and grind on his dick. 40 Cal eyed every move that Krazy made before deciding to put on his blindfold. She then moved onto 40 and began to give him some attention. 40 Cal smiled and loved every minute of it.

His moment of pleasure came to a halt when she stood up, and walked over to the table with the handcuffs. She swung them around her finger as she walked back over to Slick and 40 and cuffed their hands behind their backs. It was now time to move onto phase two of our plan.

"So have you been a bad boy today." Krazy said as she was rubbing on Slick's shoulders. "Naw I been a good boy" Slick licked his lips and smiled. "How 'bout you? You been kinda quiet for someone who wanted to be all in this pussy?" She asked as she walked over to 40 Cal. "Naw ma it ain't like that, I just ain't down for this type of shit…" 40 replied.

"Aww baby, you hurting my feelings." She said as she straddled his lap. "But I know how to make you feel me" She continued as she started to grind on him. "All of me" She whispered in his ear while nibbling on it.

Krazy

I signaled for Gutta to come over and move the boys so they could be facing each other, and that's when the fun began! I pulled down each of their pants and slowly pulled their boxers down exposing their hard and pulsating manhood. I stooped down in between them and went to work while I sucked off Slick and jacked 40 off at the same damn time. I then switched it up and had them begging for my pussy, but little did they know, before they could even enter my pussy walls they was going to experience something a little bit better than pleasure... they were going to experience PAIN.

<u>Gutta</u>

Just standing there watching Krazy wrap her lips around that man's dick shouldn't have turn me on but damn it was... In a sick way. She gazed deep into my eyes the whole time her head was bobbing up and down. She stood up and kissed them both in the mouth and bit down on Slick's tongue causing him to scream in pain, but he kept begging for more. She slapped and beat them with a paddle till the point she had these nigga's black and blue! She circled around them so calm but yet seductive, talking nasty to them to keep their interest and not to expect anything. That's when she pulled out her blade and started to make fine cuts into 40 Cal's skin.

"Aye bitch! Now this shit is getting too painful" 40 Cal yelled out.

"I'm not liking your tone." She said as she began to dig the knife in his shoulder blade. "Look you

crazy bitch, let me go!" 40 screamed out in pain.
"Aww baby, you ain't having fun anymore." She said
sweetly, like she was concerned. "Mann, what you
doin' to my nigga doe?" Slick asked.

"Oh nothing that I wouldn't do to you baby."
Krazy said innocently. "Aw nigga, stop being a pussy
and take some pain" Slick laughed in response. 40
exploded in anger "Mothafucka! She over here--" He
started, but was abruptly interrupted.

<u>Krazy</u>

Before he could get a word out I covered his mouth and slit his throat. Ain't no way in hell he was going to fuck this plan up just because he couldn't take the pain. Plus I was having too much fun.

"No no no, you can't tell him what's going on, or you're going to ruin the surprise! And since you was such a bad boy, now you have to wait 'til momma get finish with Slick" I explained. "That's what I'm talking about!" Slick said proudly.

I smiled as I walked over to Slick and sat on his lap. I rubbed the blade up and down his chest causing him to flinch and ask why the blade was so wet. Yet, I just ignored him. I sliced him on the side of his face drawing all over his skin with my blade, he screamed for me to stop but I just laughed. His womanizing ass would never get a chance to stroke in another bitch pussy when I get done with him.

He cried out to his friend who was long past dead, so I figured he should at least look at his partner before I ended his life. I walked over to 40's body and waited for Gutta to remove Slick's blindfold. When he looked at me I could have just cried laughing, the look of horror in his eyes as he saw his partner slumped over in the chair was priceless!

"You crazy bitch! What da fuck you do to my nigga, when I..." Slick started to say when I busted out in laughter to the point of tears streaming down my face.

"When you do what? Get out of your handcuffs?" I challenged.

"Bitch you think this a game! I'm well known in these streets they going to be looking for yo ass." Slick yelled as he struggled against the handcuffs.

"And I will be waiting; you think I'm scared of you Street Legends mothafucka? Yeah, I know exactly who you are. Y'all straight pussy in this bitch! You guys walk around like you some Kings, but you don't know the real meaning of puttin' in work. You walk around here flaunting everything you got like you won't get touched. But nigga I'm the bitch that will. You think yo' boss going to give a fuck that two of his soldiers are dead? Ha!' Get over yo' self nigga!" I walked over to him and sat on his lap and bit down on his ear and whispered, "Say hello to 40 Cal and let him know that I had a great time with you guys…"

And with that, I stuck my knife deep into his stomach and twisted it, slicing his spinal cord. Blood drained from his body. As he choked on his own blood, his life slowly drained from his body. I couldn't help but smile in satisfaction. I turned and faced Gutta while looking down at my blood stained hands. I heard my heart thumping in my chest loudly;

my adrenaline was still pumping through my veins. I walked up to Gutta and threw my arms around his neck and kissed him so passionately. He picked me up and walked me over to the lounge chair and began to rip my clothes off.

I untied his hair and pulled it forcing his head to tilt back as I bit down on his neck and nibble all the way up to his ear. He let out loud groans as he gripped my ass with his muscular hands. I tore open his shirt causing the buttons to pop off and pulled him on top of me. He entered me with a quick thrust and rammed his manhood inside of me. Tears rolled down my face when he hit my g-spot. He flipped me over and licked me from my ass to the top of my shoulder blades, making me quiver from the chills that swept over my body. He was stroking so deep in my pussy I swore he was hitting my cervix! He was slapping my ass so hard I yelped out in pain but yet it felt so good. We both climaxed together and laid on the lounge chair breathless.

After our wonderful session, Gutta and I took a chainsaw and chopped up both Slick and 40 Cal's body. After that, we burned the bodies to ensure that there would be no evidence left of their death.

After taking a quick shower at Gutta's house I drove my car back to my house. Thoughts of what just happened between me and Gutta filled my mind. No matter how much I try to deny it, I felt myself falling hard for him. I have fallen so hard for Gutta that it makes me sick! I'm no better than Kris's two-timing ass and the fact that I'm actually enjoy doing it, makes it even worse!

I pulled into the driveway and leaned on the steering wheel as the tears rolled down my face. I knew what I had to do but my heart didn't want me to. How could I let things get so far? Not only am I in love with Kris, I'm also in love with Gutta! I wiped my tears away before I walked into the house and went straight to the bedroom. Only to see Kris lying in the bed fast asleep. I stood there and looked at him as he slept so peacefully, and that's when I made my decision. From this day forward I'm going to stay true to Kris and distance myself from Gutta.

CHAPTER 3: YOU WIN ONE, YOU LOSE ONE

<u>Krazy</u>

Finally the time came for Kris to leave for Atlanta and I was so sad and upset that I couldn't even go to the airport with him. We said our long and drawn out goodbyes on the porch as Smooth and the other Hot Boyz members pulled up. I stood there as Kris hopped into the truck and gave me that priceless smile before they pulled off.

I sat in the living room rockin' Kris's old white tee with tear drenched eyes. Rubbing my stomach, I've been feeling sick for the past few months, but I had to fight through it all since there was business that needed to be handled. From staking out and making blueprints of the locations, to planning out the hits.

There simply was no time to make doctor appointments just to be told that I'm coming down with a common cold. With all the late night planning Gutta and I had coming up, taking a sick day wasn't an option.

I laid down on the couch feeling dizzy, when a sudden knock came at the screen door. I looked over at the door only to see Gutta through the glass. For the past couple of months, I have avoided any alone moments with Gutta. The only time we was around each other was for business purposes only. I know he noticed my avoidant demeanor, but he never said a word about it. Even though he respected my space, my heart and my body still yearned for him.

I slowly walked over to the door and let him in. Without even making eye contact with him, I went back to the couch to lay down. Gutta sat down in the chair directly across from me and looked at me for a second before opening his mouth.

"You aiight young thang?" "Yeah I'm good" I said as I sat up. "You sure? You ain't looking too hot." He asked again with concern. "Naw I'm good I promise." I said frankly.

"Look, if you ain't feeling good then you need to let me know, because we can do this hit another day..." Gutta said as he got up and sat next to me. "Naw, we have to do this shit now because we put this hit off for a whole month, and we just can't take any more chances. I'm pretty sure that Red is on to something since we knocked off Slick and 40 cal." I explained.

"Yeah I get that. But yo' health comes first, and we can handle it another day." Gutta replied as he began to hold my hand. Yet I quickly snatched my hand back. "My health is none of your concern. We have business to handle, and I can't let my health cause us to delay this hit any longer! I can do this, I been doing this shit all my life and now that Kris is gone, I have to handle it and hold things down for him 'till he get back."

Gutta quickly stood up. "So that's what's this is about? You so worried about this nigga and his expectations that yo health is the last thing on your mind!" He shouted. "Yeah what did you expect? He is my boyfriend and more importantly he is my family Gutta! So me not holding things down isn't an option." I rebutted.

"Man I been biting my tongue for so long, but I see that someone needs to open up yo eyes, I get the fact that you trying to play this loyal girlfriend role but what type of nigga up and jump state and leave his bitch to handle all his dirty work for him?" Gutta said obviously upset.

"You might look at him like he's leaving me to handle his 'dirty work', but I look at it like he's trusting his partner to get the job done! I know you don't get it and I don't expect you to, but I love him and he loves me and this is just how we are, this is how we handle business! And don't forget we are paying you for your service, so I don't see why you are complaining or have shit to say about anything! What gives you the right to speak on him that way?" I yelled in irritation.

Gutta shook his head before speaking, "You just don't get it do you? I can give two fucks about what the hell y'all paying me. Shit I'm already paid with or without ya'll chump change! The only reason I stayed this long was for you! You are too good of a woman to be hanging around that wack ass nigga! You sitting here with blood on you mothafuckin' hands and what does this nigga have? Right not a damn thing he get a first class trip to ATL while he leave you to fend for your fuckin' self on these streets."

"He only left me here because I can handle my own! And he trust me to handle it the right way." I replied as I crossed my arms. "Are you fucking delusional? Or does this nigga just got you brain washed? You here and he is there, sounds like he going on a Hot Boyz vacation to me! Who just leave they partner behind? Come on Krazy use yo' fucking head!" Gutta snapped.

"Like I said, we been doing this shit way before you pop in the picture! Like honestly you ain't even know who the fuck I was before this mission!" I said not backing down.

Gutta laughed in response. "Young thang I know more about you than you know about yourself...You know these streets talk."

"Ok yea the streets be talking but I don't know why you sweatin' me anyway. Like honestly you think I wasn't going to notice that you have a chick? I saw all her shit in yo' bathroom at yo crib! So where did you expect this to go? You got a woman and I have a man so this thing between us is done!" I spat.

"So you telling me you ain't feel shit between us? You telling me that at night you think about this nigga?" Gutta said as he got close to my face. "You telling me every time I put this dick all up in yo' mothafucking guts that you had that nigga yo mind?" He asked while grabbing both of my arms and pulling me closer to him urging me for my answer.

I pushed him out my face in disgust at the fact that he was right about everything. "Get the fuck out my face with that shit! And no I don't think about him when I'm with you but that ain't the point! What we was doing was wrong, and doing shit like that ain't goin' to get us nowhere."

Gutta began to calm down and sat back on the couch. "It can go anywhere you want it to go. It's all on you young thang. From day one I saw something in you that I wanted and I ain't goin to stop till I get it."

"At this point in the game I can't even think about a future with you, I think it's best for you to let go whatever feelings you have for me and move on with yo girl, whoever that bitch might be." I rolled my eyes as I turned my head away from him. "Naw I don't think so young thang, you'll come around. But yeah, be ready round midnight to do this hit." Gutta said as he stood up and walked out the door.

I stood there as he walked out the door and I was just speechless. I never wanted to string Gutta feelings along but we both needed to be realistic with ourselves. All this shit needed to be put to the side so we can focus on this business that we had to handle! And when it all said and done, I can move on to the next assignment on the list, and he can do the same forgetting about all about me. Falling in love with Gutta was never a part of the plan, shit if it wasn't for Smooth urging Kris to add on a free agent, this shit would have never happened!

I walked upstairs into my bedroom and laid onto the bed, staring up at the ceiling wondering what the fuck did this night have in store for me? Man I pray this sickness goes away so I can get on with this mission.

I slept the day away 'til my phone rung and of course it was Gutta. I hopped out of the bed and washed up before putting on my black dickie pants and my black hoodie. I slipped on my black J's and grabbed my car keys before hopping into my all black caprice classic. I sped down the highway to the strip joint called All Stars, where Red, our next target, worked.

When I pulled up to the place I slowed down and noticed how crowded it was, but shit what could expect on a Saturday! I quickly pulled around to the side of the building and parked my whip. Pulling my gun out the glove compartment, I tucked it in my pants before I walked around to the back of the club to meet up with Gutta.

When I got to the back, he was already there standing smoking a black and sexy as fuck. My body's reaction to his sex appeal irritated my soul! As I looked him up and down, I must say he dressed to impress! He was rockin' an orange polo with the dark True Religion jeans, and the fitted cap to match. His all white Al Wissam jacket was looking fresh to death. I snapped out of lustful trance when he flashed a smile at me, causing me to notice that he changed his grill up to his gold grill with the yellow canary diamonds in it.

"Aight young thang you ready?" He asked nonchalantly. "Yeah" I replied curtly. "Aight hopefully this goes as planned, and I can get her out here without her suspecting a thing." He continued. "Aight I'm waiting on you, let's get this shit over with cause its cold as fuck out here." I said shivering in my mere hoodie. "I got you young thang." Gutta said as he quickly kissed me on the forehead.

Gutta

I walked into the spot chuckling a little bit at the face the Krazy made. Yet it was time to get back to business. I made my way through the club like I ran that shit! I got me a c booth in the corner and waited until I saw ole girl Red walk out and did her number on the stage. She was swirling all around that pole, bouncin' and clappin' dat' ass. I waved that big faced bill as she walked over to my table with her hands on her hips.

"I hope you don't think a hundred dollars is worth my service." Red snapped. "Naw baby girl that was just so I could get your attention, believe me, it's more where that came from." I hinted, causing Red to smile. "That's what's up. So what you need" She said as she sat down on my lap.

"Naw baby girl it ain't what I need it's what I want. A nice young stallion like you shouldn't be in this place working, you should be in a nice ass crib tending to a man like me, getting dicked down every night like a real woman should. And I believe you the one I need in my corner." I said, sweet talking her to the point that she blushed.

"Oh really?" She asked. "Yes really. So how bout you change up outta them clothes and I take you out somewhere nice tonight and treat you like a queen." I licked my lips to seal the deal. "Aight, wait for me by the stairs." Red said seductively before she switched her way to the changing room.

Krazy

I stood there outside freezing my ass off when my phone started to ring; I look down at my phone and saw the text message from Gutta telling me to get ready. I looked around for a place to hide so I ducked down behind a dumpster, and watched the door waiting for Gutta to appear. Within minutes, Gutta walked out with Red laughing like they were having a good time. She was smiling so hard while she had her arm wrapped around his. She truly had no clue what was going to happen next.

Gutta made eye contact with me before give me a head nod, so I pulled out my gun and cocked it when all of a sudden, everything turned into slow motion. As Gutta removed his arm from Red's grasp, he pushed her in front of him and swiftly pulled out his glock, but as he pulled the trigger, his gun jammed!

My heart dropped to the pit of my stomach, it wasn't even time for me to react I was so shock that right in front of my eyes that our plan was unraveling. Red look down the barrel of the gun before turning around running into a full sprint as she tried to escape out of the back parking lot. I stood up and without even thinking, rushed towards her and wrestler her to the ground. I cold cocked her in the back of her head but still able to move, she rolled over and fought me for the gun. And at that moment, a sharp pain hit me in my stomach, my head started to spin and my vision started to get blurry.

Gutta

I stood there trying to unjam my gun when I saw Red knee Krazy in her stomach. Krazy fell over onto the ground holding her stomach, while Red scrambled to her feet and started to stomp Krazy to the point she let out shrieks of pain and agony. She coughed up blood as she tried to defend herself. I finally got my gun to work and with the bullet in the chamber I aimed right between Red eyes' for an instant kill shot, and she was out like a light. I rushed to Krazy's side and held her in my arms.

"Krazy look at me you okay?" I yelled as I grabbed her face towards me. "Oh my gosh! I don't know what wrong! It hurts so bad" She said, as she held her stomach wincing in pain. I quickly picked her up off the ground. "I'mma take you to the hospital ok?" I stated. Krazy began to plead. "No! I don't wanna go to the hospital just take..."She blacked out before she could finish her sentence.

I made my way over to her car and placed her in the passenger seat. When I shut the door I looked down and noticed the blood all over my hands. Damn, she was losing a lot of blood but why? I hopped in the car and sped to the nearest hospital where they rushed her back to the ER. I sat in the waiting room filling out the paperwork to the best of my ability.

I grew impatient as I was waiting to hear from the doctor, when the nurse finally told me I could go see her. I practically ran back to Krazy's room where she laid in the hospital bed asleep, looking like an angel. I gripped my fist as I walked over to her side of the bed, and held her hand. How could I be so stupid and let her get hurt like that? The plan was so well thought out, that I didn't even expect it to unfold like that. My thoughts were interrupted when the doctor walked in with his chart, and checked Krazy's vitals before turning to me.

"Well it look like she's going to be okay, even though she lost a lot of blood. I'm sorry to have to inform you sir that the baby didn't make it..." The Doctor explained. "The baby?" I asked in confusion. "Yes, you didn't know your girlfriend was pregnant?" The Doctor asked in shock. "No sir I did not!" I said, looking over at Krazy. "Well that's funny, she should have known by now since she was almost three months" The Doctor replied. Sadness took over me. "No she never told me, to be honest sir I don't think she knew."

"Well, if you want I can tell her when she wakes up." He suggested. "Naw, I'll tell her myself." I sighed.

Without another word said, the doctor left out the room and left me standing there like an idiot. How could I've not noticed that she was pregnant? Why didn't she tell me? Could it have been mine and she didn't want to tell me? All of these questions filled my head as I took a seat next to her bed and laid my head on her lap and fell asleep.

Meanwhile:

<u>The Mysterious Man</u>

I stood there in the crowd behind the crime scene tape, looking at the horrific scene in the parking lot of All Stars strip club; only to see part time lover spread out on the cold cement. Blood was everywhere and people was huddled together to keep warm while being nosy. I walked closer to scope the scene myself, the police stood there examining her body while looking lost at the same time.

My blood boiled as I heard the police Chief say that it must have been a mugging gone wrong. The police was all over the place, but these damn investigators getting paid to do detective work couldn't even tell that this was gang related. The specks of blood around her body clearly showed some type of struggle and that she was murdered by someone professional. And that someone have been hot on my tail for years. Ha, I knew he would come for me, but not like this...this nigga straight killed my main bitch. But just like how he's tracking me, I've been tracking him. It shouldn't be long before he comes for me and when he does I will be waiting.

<u>Krazy</u>

When I awoke, I looked around the unfamiliar room that I was in. I instantly got nervous because the last thing I remember, I was laying in Gutta's arms in the parking lot in so much pain then everything went blank. I looked around and lifted my arm up to notice all the IVs in my arm. Damn I'm in the hospital! What the hell? I don't even know how long I was out?

My mind was racing from one thought to the next. I looked over to my right and noticed Gutta sitting in the chair with his head down on my lap. He look so peaceful. I reached over and rubbed his dreads lightly to wake him up. When he lifted his head up, I could see that his eyes were bloodshot red like he had been crying and his nose was red. I sat there and looked at him and my heart just melted. He gave me that priceless smile before he grabbed my hand and rubbed it.

"Hey young thang, how you feeling?" He said sweetly. "I'm feeling ok I guess, how long was I out?" I inquired. "Just for a couple of hours" He said. "Damn that bitch must have really done a number on me huh?" I laughed, but Gutta just looked at me seriously before speaking. "Yeah....you lost a lot of blood." "Damn foreal!" I exclaimed. "Umm, can I ask you something?" He asked curiously with a straight face.

"Yeah what's wrong?" I said, as I slowly sat up in the bed, trying to read his reaction.

"How long was you feeling sick?" He asked. "Well, not that long it just started a couple of weeks ago" I shrugged. "Are you sure?" He posed. "Yeah I'm sure. Why?" I asked, not really getting where this conversation is going.

Gutta looked me deeply in the eyes before speaking. "Krazy, I really don't know how to say this, but I'm just going to keep it real, the doctor said you was about three months pregnant and that was the reason for you losing so much blood."

"Pregnant? What the fuck!" I lashed out in confusion. "You ain't even know?" Gutta said flustered.

The emotions hit me out of nowhere as I held my stomach, and tears started to form in my eyes. "Is the baby ok?" I asked Gutta with pleading eyes. Hoping he would say the answer I yearned for.

"Naw young thang," he sighed as he choked out the words. "The baby didn't make it…" "How the fuck could I be so stupid and reckless! It's all my fault!" I cried hysterically. Gutta stood up and embraced me. "No it's not your fault! You didn't know."

"But I should have known! I was sick as hell and didn't even think to check. And I was so worried about this bullshit, that I didn't even know I was having a baby!" I yelled out in anger at myself for stupidity. "I'm fucking stupid!"

"It's going to be alright Krazy I'm here and I'm goin' to help you through this." Gutta said as he consoled me.

I just sat there in Gutta's arms crying, I was hurt about the baby not making it but I was more upset with myself because the baby could have been the child that Kris and I made together, and now that Kris is gone and the baby is gone and I'm left all alone ! The child that could have made us one is now gone forever!

I stayed in the hospital one more night before they released me. I gathered my things and walked out of the hospital with Gutta by my side. He never left me the whole two days I was there except to run to my crib and get me some clothes since the ones I had was bloody and clearly needed to be thrown in the trash. Gutta finally brought me home and stayed there with me for 6 days.

"Well you can put yo' clothes in the guest room if you like" Gutta suggested. "Well where else would I put them?" I said sarcastically with a smirk on my face, causing him to chuckle in response.

I laughed to myself as walked into the guest room and started to put my things away. As soon as I was done, I sat on the bed and looked around. And I must say, he has great taste in furniture. I laid across the king size bed and it felt like I was laying on nothing but clouds. I look around the room at the Egyptian décor and felt like I was a Nubian queen! I quickly dozed off into a nice slumber, all this moving and the emotions I've been going through for the past weeks had me exhausted.

I woke up later that evening and walked down the stairs only to see Gutta sitting on his black leather L-couch with the fireplace going. He was sipping out of a bottle of Remy looking like he was going through it. I guess I wasn't the only one that had issues going on. I stood in the entryway into the living room and looked at him. Even in his sad state he was still fine, with his dreads hanging down sweeping his collarbone, in a white beater and black sweatpants. He looked over at me and gave me his little smirk before speaking.

"Hey, I see you finally decided to get up." He greeted. "Yeah, I was so tired" I replied. "You know there is some food in the kitchen if you hungry." He informed. "Naw, I'm good." I said as I walked into the living room. "Aight, just let me know if you need anything" He reassured, as I sat next to him. "I'm good, but it looks like you need something..." I hinted.

"Like what?" He said with his deep voice as he licked his lips and lustfully gazed at me. "Nothing like that nasty!" I laughed as I playfully pushed. "It looks like you need someone to talk to, you look like you have a lot on yo mind." I continued. "If only you knew" Gutta replied.

"Well tell me about it then." I suggested. "Oh so you wanna know 'bout me huh?" He smiled. "Yeah why not? Shit, I don't even know yo' government name! Shit you could be a serial rapist and I'm living in yo' crib!" I laughed.

"I wouldn't do anything to you unless you wanted me to. My mom brought me up better than that." Gutta said. "You hardly ever speak on yo mother." I commented.

"Yeah I know, cause she dead." He said, causing a moment of silence to sweep over the room. I automatically felt bad. "I'm sorry...I didn't--" I started but was cut off by Gutta. "You good young thang, it's not like you knew or anything." "Well don't feel bad cause my parents are dead." I added, to relieve the awkwardness in the room. "Well I never knew my father and my mother was murdered..." His voice trailed off. "Oh my gosh!" I replied in shock.

"Yeah. My life ain't no fairy tale. Half these nigga's today can't walk a mile in my shoes. That's why I walk alone; that's why when I do my job I do it on the solo tip because no one can be trusted. Not even the one you love." Gutta began.

<u>Gutta</u>

I began to finally explain my story to Krazy. Something I never done with anybody on this earth. But, I knew we were cut from the same cloth, so it's only right to share it with the woman who holds my heart.

Flashback:

I was born Shakeer Lamal Davis to my young twenty year old mother, Francis, better known as Frankie. The way I remember my mom was how fun and loving she was, but she had a temper and would kick yo' ass in a heartbeat. I never knew too much about my dad and my mom never brought him up, shit, for all I know he might be six feet under somewhere. But my mom wasn't your typical mother, she was a leader, she was the bosses of all bosses.

She ran the north side of Detroit with an iron fist. My mother was the head of the Street Legends gang. She was the one who started the whole organization. Most of the members who currently are there at the top now, started at the bottom back then. She was the one telling them where to drop and who to cut. But my mom always gave back to her people though. She walked with authority, she demanded respect, and if you or anyone wanted war she gave them Armageddon.

My mother taught me everything I know. At the age of 14, I knew the ends and outs of the streets, my mom gave me my first gun at 15 and boy learning how to shoot a sniper rifle was like a boot camp in itself. She always told me if you don't get them with one shot then I'm no good to nobody. I loved my mom; I cherished everything she taught me. She never sold me dreams, she always kept it real. We lived in a dog eat dog world and there's so many people that's out there to take you out.

My mom trained me how to be the ultimate tracker, and hit man out here in the Detroit area. See back in those days, people walked out in pure daylight and killed a nigga on the spot. My mom was on point, she realized that the times was changing and she had to prepare her one man army. Consists of only me... I was all she had and she was all I had.

That cold February night was the coldest one I have ever felt. I just finished one of my missions and I was to report back to the headquarters to escort my mother out to her car. Yet, when I walked in the main office it reeked with the smell of blood. I pushed open the double doors, only to see my mother sprawled out over her desk naked. Blood dripped off her desk onto her all white fur rug. The closer I got the more the rage and sadness filled in my heart, they cut her wrist and they shot her right between her eyes. A straight kill shot. Whoever killed her was making a statement and that statement was clear. It was war!

I found my mother's clothes that were ripped off her. I dressed her like she was a newborn baby, the same way she did for me when I was young. I carried her to her lounge chair in her office and laid her down. She didn't deserve to be exposed like that; I closed her eyelids and kissed her for the last time, before walking out the office with my mind made up. The way my mom was killed was unforgivable and I promised to myself and as well to my mother, that I would track her killer down and take my seat on the throne over the empire that my mother built.

I moved in with my grandmother who took care of me, but from the sidelines I watched the empire that my mother built crumble at the hands of her so called loyal workers. Half of them are dead but a few remained. The ones she trusted didn't even show up at her funeral! I was filled with rage and I wanted revenge. I wanted to kill that motherfucker who took the only one who loved me away. The closer I got to him or her it seem like they was ten steps ahead of me. I know that they are out there and I know they're waiting for me, but I been watching my steps since that day. I kept a low profile; I went to school and keep my grades up so that I graduated with honors. I have a clean record and kept out of the public eyes. And most importantly I kept my business to myself.

I never had to worry about money because every penny my mother earned was mine. So I guess you could say I was hood rich, but the money never mattered to me. I make a couple of moves for nigga's in the streets to keep my pockets on swole. I only fuck with the nigga's that keep their business A-one, cause these wack ass nigga's today run their mouths too much. But on my down time I kept a good bitch on my side but lately I been slipping with this thing us humans call love. When I love someone I love them hard, I treat my women like the queens that they are and never judge them, cause who am I to judge anyone.

Krazy

I sat there as Gutta told me all his secrets. I was amazed at how calm he was, no tears no nothing... like he was empty on the inside. The way he talks about his mother I would have expected some type of emotion, but all I saw was anger in his eyes like this happened yesterday. Sadly, I could relate to that. It seems like everything he been through I was just experiencing. I lost a lot too and I'm still haunted by it, but I could feel myself getting cold hearted almost like I was lifeless in some kind of way, I looked at him and didn't even utter a word, but he still went on, telling the story about this mysterious girl he was fucking with.

Gutta

Flashback:

Yeah, the girl I'm fucking with gave me that feeling like she was the one. I met her at a party out there on the eastside. Everybody was there all the big time movers and shakers, yet I was in the crib handling business trying to get some info on a nigga on this mission I was working on. That was when she walked in the door. She seemed so confident like she ran the place. She wore a light denim mini skirt with a yellow tube top with the heels to match. She eyed me the whole time before she made her move. The way she talked and carried herself reminded me so much of my mother, that I couldn't let her slip through my fingers.

Yet, as the months went by our relationship seemed to change and I really started to see who she really was. She really wasn't from the streets. Hell! That bitch never got her hands dirty a day in her life! She grew up in Southfield in a nice middle class home with both of her parents. A spoiled little princess, that's what she was. Everything she wanted mommy and daddy gave it to her. It tripped me outta my mind because she acted like she was a real hood bitch. The way she talked about the streets made it seem like she had been through some shit but really she was just like the rest. Looking for a nigga to take care of her while she laid on her back. Like her pussy was golden. It took me awhile to catch on to her true intention, because the bitch had me gone for a minute. She went to school in the city, she kept the house in tip top shape, bitch was holding it down in the bedroom, she even invited a couple of her girlfriends over to show a nigga a good time. But the time came for her to put her money where her mouth, was when I took her out on a hit with me.

I gave her a gun. I made sure everything was mapped out. I even went over the plan with her over and over again! At the end of the day, she almost got me kilt! She didn't even know how to shoot a gun, let alone hold one! She was so scared I thought she was going to piss on herself. From that day, on I keep that bitch at arm's length. She did her thang and I did mine, sometimes she wouldn't even come home for weeks, and I could care less.

I sat there telling Krazy my whole life story. Everything I could think off I told her and that's when it hit me. The bitch I was with and thought I loved, everything I wanted that night at the party, was Krazy! Everything that bitch was trying to be was right here in front of my eyes. I found the one I've been looking for. We stayed up and talked for hours, until Krazy fell asleep on the couch. I picked her up and carried her to the master bedroom. I laid her in the bed and climbed in next to her. I held her as I dozed off for some much need rest.

<u>Krazy</u>

The next couple of months spent with Gutta could only be described as a dream. With everything that's been going on Gutta and I decided that it would be best if we held off on the big mission and focused on other things. Coming to that decision it felt like it was some weight lifted off my shoulders, since I was still dealing with the loss of my unborn child and the unknown whereabouts of Kris. To get my mind off all that bullshit I immersed myself in Hot Boyz affiliated work. I wasn't really up for the killing and shit so I focused more on the financial aspects of the crew.

Sitting in my room with all the paperwork spread across the bed I thumb through everything to make sure our money was adding up when Gutta appeared in my doorway. Gutta stood there looking at me lying across the bed before letting his presence be known. "Hey there young thang what you up to?" He asked before walking towards my bed. I look up at him with a smile on my face before simply replying, "Just handling this money for the Hot Boyz."

He stood there for a moment before sitting on my bed, "Fasho well how about when you done with that we go out?" "Go out where?" I asked puzzled but yet curiously, "You know go out to a movies, dinner, drinks..."Like a date?" I asked sarcastically before sitting up in the bed. "Yea a date, you know something you do with your man" Gutta replied with a little laugh." I never went on a date before." "Seriously?" Gutta responded unbelievingly. "Yeah, to be honest taking this little break on the hit is something new to me as well." I answered honestly.

"So when did you and Kris spend your down time?" Gutta ask nonchalantly, I sat there and let out a small laugh because Gutta speaking Kris name is shocking since I knew he really didn't care too much about Kris. Sitting there really thinking about our down time I finally answered Gutta "I guess our down time was when we did our stakeouts or whenever the Hot Boyz was doing a party or something." As soon as I finished my sentence a confident but yet cool smile appeared across Gutta's face before stating "Well today we going to do everything you never experienced before".

I sat there on the bed and smiled just at the thought of actually going on a date, just thinking about my date with Gutta made me realize that Kris and I really didn't do anything but work! The only thing I can think of that Kris and I did together outside of work during the day was grocery shopping. But that was all behind me now and I quickly rushed through my paperwork just so I could start preparing for my date. After a nice hot shower, I looked through my belongings and got dressed in a simple strapless black dress, with some black thigh high boots to match. I let my hair hang down as it flowed past my shoulder blades.

I walked out into the living putting on my leather coat as Gutta stood smiling ear to ear as he observed my attire. Without a moment to waste, we hopped into his car and hit the town for a day of fun. Even with a simple date at the movies, and grabbing a bite to eat, I was filled with so much joy. To end a perfect day we watched the sun set on the Detroit River walk and cuddled together to keep warm. As we made our way home, Gutta concluded the night with much need passion as we rolled around in the sheets moaning and groaning in pure bliss until we reached our peaks together and fell to sleep with our bodies still intertwined.

<u>Gutta</u>

A month went by and Krazy and I seem to be getting along well, but with all these phone calls from these bitches coming in I could tell that Krazy was starting to feel uneasy. Our conversations became strained. The once blissful smiles turned into scowls. With all this tension between us, I could never find the right moment to reassure her that the bitches on my line weren't important to me. Matter of fact, I believe I made it worse by pushing the bitches to voice mail. My love for Krazy was endless but with the fact that both of us never confessed our feelings out loud for one another made us question our value for each other.

That night while we were getting ready to go to bed, I sat on my side of the bed and looked at all the text messages in my phone. The moment I went to reply to the one of the messages my phone vibrated in my hand. I looked around; making sure Krazy was out of the room before I answered. "Hello" I said in almost a whisper, "Why the fuck you whispering?" The voice of the random female I used to fuck with yelled through the phone.

"Look stop blowing my phone up!" I responded in annoyance. "What the fuck you mean stop blowing your phone up? You can't fuck with a bitch now cause you over there cuffed up or something?" She ranted, not giving me a chance to speak. In that instant, Krazy walk into the bedroom with her arms crossed glaring at me before snapping, "Who the fuck you on the phone with!"

I hung up the phone and turned to look at her, sighing deeply. I knew that this conversation would not end well I decided to answer her honestly. "Man it was some bitch I used to fuck with back in the day." Krazy stomped over to the bed so she could be in my face, and began to fuss "What the fuck you mean a bitch you use to fuck with? Clearly you still fucking with the bitch, if she still calling you every motherfuckin' day!" Krazy started to poke me in my chest, as she continued. "You think I'm fucking stupid Gutta, you stay pushing people to voice mail and sneaking around texting and talking on the phone like I wouldn't fucking find out!" "Let me see yo' fuckin phone and if she is just some random bitch from the past!" I challenged. "No! What the fuck I gotta do that for?" I said firmly. "What you mean no? You betta' give me yo' phone" She yelled.

<u>Krazy</u>

"Give you my phone? What the fuck you mean? You ain't my bitch doe' " Gutta snapped, causing me to stare at him in disbelief. "So what are we then?

Why the fuck am I living with you wasting my mothafuckin' time if we ain't shit!" I yelled in anger.

"You know what fuck this, fuck this house, and fuck you with yo' bitchass! I'm out this bitch!" I screamed as I walked out the bedroom and stormed out the house, slamming the door behind me. I walked down the street steaming with anger. How could something so perfect change to shit overnight? Damn, why does this keep happening to me? So many thoughts filled my head as I walked down towards the main street. By the time I gained awareness, I looked around only to realize that I was in an area that I was not familiar with. What the hell? And it was getting late too? Damn this is not a good look for my ass. I sighed in defeat as I walked into the nearest liquor store. Without even looking, I bumped right into a man's chest. I looked up, only to see the infamous Pistol.

He had an on black V-neck tee that revealed his tatted up collar bone and muscular arms. He hovered over me with his 6'4 frame, and gazed at me in confusion as I looked back at him embarrassed at the fact that I came out the house looking a hot ass mess. My hair was in a messy high bun, rocking a red tank top, with the Minnie mouse pajama shorts and slippers to match. "Krazy? You aiight? What the fuck happened to you?" He bombarded me with questions, but all I could do was shake my head and held back the tears. I was speechless. "Did you walk all the way out here?" He asked. I finally shook my head yes, and he sucked his teeth in response. "Man, whatever the fuck is goin', I can't have you out here looking like this, let's go." He said as he snatched my arm up, like a brother with his little sister, and led me to his car.

He quickly opened the car door of his black and chrome charger. I sat in his passenger seat and watched as he made his way over to the driver side. It was perfect timing because the rain began to pour like hell outside. If it wasn't for him, my crazy ass would be outside walking in it.

Pistol pulled up to the house Kris and I shared. Escorting me into the house, Pistol stayed by my side making sure I made it in safely. We sat on the couch and caught up. "What are you doing out here? I thought you were in Atlanta?" I asked. "I was until Liyah called me and told me she needed more manpower. I heard it's been an all-out war since you been doing those hits on the Street Legends." Pistol explained. "Oh yeah" I said nonchalantly, even though I knew my ass has been all up in Gutta that I forgot all about the Street Legends. "Yeah, so we'll be having a meeting soon to get things back on track, but damn seeing you out here walking and shit got me concerned." Pistol said, staring into my eyes.

Out of all the Hot Boyz, Pistol was the most calm, and caring one. He was like a big brother to me and was always a listening ear. I stared back at him, and couldn't help but finally notice how fine he really was. Looking like a spitting image the sexy LL Cool J, I could understand why all the women would drop their drawls when they laid eyes on him. Yet, this was not the time to have these thoughts. I'm just fortunate that he was there at the right place and at the right time.

"I'll be aiight. Just had a lot on my mind and needed take a walk." I explained. "Yeah, aight!" Pistol started. "Well, if you ever need to talk, just know that I'm here for you baby girl. Just don't be doin' no stupid shit like taking long walks at night in your pajamas." He joked, causing me to laugh in response.

"Aiight! I won't." I reassured. "Good! But I got to meet up with Liyah, so just be ready for that call about the meeting." Pistol said as he stood up and made his way to the front door. "Ok, I'll be ready." I replied before escorting him out. Now I was finally alone. Back at the original house I shared with Kris. I took a deep sigh before lying on my couch, and letting the tears cascade down my face. Once again, this was another lesson learned. These men out here ain't loyal, and in this game, the only person I need to be loyal to is my damn self! And at that moment, I vowed to do just that.

Weeks passed as I made no attempt to contact Gutta, after all we been through together to have him say those words to me left a big hole in my heart. The only way I knew to forget about this pain was to indulge myself with Hot Boyz affiliated business. I been so cooped up with Gutta that I didn't realize how much work was piling up, after contacting Liyah we set up a meeting at my crib for we can get shit in order.

That night Samya, Liyah, and Pistol met up at the crib and we started to conduct the meeting. On and off during the meeting my phone rang but instead of answering I pushed it to voice mail without a second thought. We continued our conversation when a loud pounding came at my door.

In unison everyone pulled out their guns, I looked around confused thinking who in their right mind would pound on my door like that? A loud voice roared on the other side of the door. "Krazy I know yo' ass in there, come open this mothafucking door!" I sat there in my seat in disbelief to hear Gutta's voice.

I rushed to the door opening it only to see Gutta, and with a quickness I closed the front door for the crew wouldn't be able to see him. Quickly catching on to what I was trying to do, Gutta pushed the door back open while pushing his way into the house.

"Naw we ain't keepin' no secrets! Fuck these mothafuckas why should we have to hide unless you ashamed of some shit? Gutta spat as if spitting venom into my already wounded heart. "Gutta we going have to talk about this later" I said trying to diffuse the situation before it got out of hand. Unknowing, that the situation was about to go to a whole different level.

"Man fuck all that we handling this shit right now in front of all these mothafuckas! You so worried about what they think that you denying yourself what you really want. You wanna act like you someone down ass bitch, but want to hide it the next someone gets wind of what you doing. Where the fuck was these nigga's when you were going through all that shit? I know I ain't perfect but damn at least I had yo' back!" Gutta ranted.

Feeling disrespected I had to put that nigga in his place, "Last time I check I wasn't yo' bitch doe! Ain't that the bullshit you let out yo' mouth a couple weeks ago?" I revealed. "You want to play the good guy role but you just as bad as Kris with all that sneaking around with these hoes! All ya'll nigga's want a down ass bitch but don't know how to keep her! Why da fuck do every nigga expect females to be loyal when ya'll mothafuckas ain't loyal ya'll damn self!" The whole house sat in silence as I continued, "You run up in my damn house telling me I ashamed and hiding what going on between us! Ha! Nigga please how can I hide shit when you ain't even claiming a bitch? I said, as I stood there waiting for Gutta's response.

"This ain't high school a nigga don't have to sit up here and ask you to be my girlfriend. What type of fuck shit is that? I'm a grown ass man not that pussy ass nigga you are so accustomed to! Nigga if I rock with you I rock with you, ain't no secret about it! I don't let any ol' bitch live with me, I don't even cater to any old bitch! You need to step up to yo' position or get the fuck on period."

I stood there speechless with nothing to say, I mean what could you possibly say after something like that. Gutta continued to speak making his final statement. "I ain't here for games and I gave you enough time to figure out what you want to do, either you stay here with these fuck niggas or come be with a real nigga." With that, Gutta exited the house leaving everyone speechless.

Liyah was the first to interrupt the silence, "Krazy you fuckin' up! You over here stuck on dick, and got

this nigga coming up to yo' crib, interrupting a fuckin'
Hot Boyz meeting, and yo' ass let him call us a fuck
nigga? A fuck nigga!" She yelled in anger at the
disrespect.

"I don't give a fuck if you was fuckin' and suckin'
him all day long, yo' ass should never put a nigga
over the fuckin' Hot Boyz! I don't give a fuck about
yo' little love triangle. All I care about is taking out the
Street Legends and keeping the Hot Boyz at the top,
like yo' ass should be doing! Get yo' fuckin head
back in the game! Whatever you got to do to fix this
shit, you betta' do it right the fuck now! You heard
me?" Liyah commanded. Instead of snapping back at
her, I knew Liyah was talking some real ass shit. I
couldn't help but to respect it. All I could do was nod
my head in agreement.

Liyah then turned to the others. "As for the rest
of ya'll. I don't want to hear none of ya'll asses even

mentioning that fuck nigga's name, or even bringing this stupid ass shit up! What happened in this fuckin' house will stay in this fuckin house! And that's a Hot Boyz order! You hear me?" She yelled. Pistol and Samya both nodded their heads in agreement.

"Now I'm done with this shit. We will have another meeting next week. Like I said Krazy, you need to get your head in the game. Don't be bringing any more drama to a Hot Boyz meeting again." She snarled. Giving me the stare of death, Liyah grabbed her shit and stormed out my house. Samya quickly followed snickering at what just happened, as I mean mugged her ass back.

Yet, Pistol was the only one who stayed. I buried my head in my hands trying to calm my nerves as Pistol sat on the arm of my loveseat, and rubbed on my back. "I know Krazy. You had a rough ass day. It happens to the best of us. Ain't nobody perfect, we're humans. So don't beat yourself up over it." He explained, giving me some of his words of wisdom. I looked up at him holding back the tears of anger at myself.

"I fucked up Pistol." I confessed. "It's ok. We all fucked up at least once. But the key is to bounce back. Don't let this shit get you down. Just take some time and get your head back in the game. You'll be fine." He reassured me, flashing that Colgate smile. That was one thing about Pistol; he always brought the good out of any bad situation.

He gave me a hug and pecked me on the cheek before making his exit. I sat there and let his words sink in. I really did need some time to get my head back in the game. So instead of calling Gutta or worrying about Kris or anybody else for that matter, I decided to take the time out and do what Liyah told me... Get my head back in the game.

Three months passed after Gutta gave me an ultimatum to either be with him or stay with the Hot Boyz. After clearing my head, I figured we should finally talk about it. Making my way to his house, I pulled up the driveway and noticed an all pink charger parked in the spot that use to be mine. I sat in the car in disbelief. This mothafucka' bust up in my damn crib giving me ultimatums and shit while he laid up with some bitch? Rage filled my body as I grabbed the 9mm out my glove box and marched up to the front door. With one swift kick I bust the door down only to see Gutta getting his dick rode by some Mexican bitch!

"Are you fucking serious Gutta?" I yelled making my presence known. The girl scrambled off of Gutta's dick putting on her clothes as he sat up adjusting himself. "Krazy wait calm down." Gutta said as he stood up. "Nigga fuck that you up here fucking some bitch after you made a scene at my crib like you actually gave a fuck about me!" I screamed as my emotions got the best of me. I aimed my gun at that hoe ready to let my rounds off into her body as Gutta rushed me for the gun. As we struggle shots rang throughout the entire house. The bitch duck and dodged bullets as she scream in horror running out of the house.

Finally I let go of the gun before slapping the fuck out of Gutta causing spit to fly outta his mouth. My chest heaved in and out and my hands trembled as I ruthlessly slapped Gutta over and over! Instead of retaliating, Gutta just pulled me into him and held me. I don't know why I respond the way I do with him, but all I could do at this moment was cry. Not just because of what he did, but what Kris did to me, what everyone did to me. I'm so tired of being fucked over!

I pushed Gutta off me and slapped him one more good time. "I'm sick of this shit, I'm done with yo ass!" I screamed with tears still in my eyes, I turned around and left out the house. I quickly hopped in my car and pulled off.

I sat at home sipping on a bottle of vodka as my emotions got the best of me, I looked over at my phone and sulked at the fact that Gutta didn't even attempt to run after me. I quickly shook that thought out my head. Fuck that nigga! Why would his dog ass run after me? I grabbed my phone and threw it across the room. I stood up and stumbled towards the front door and onto the porch and let the summer night breeze hit my face. I looked up when some headlights pulled into my driveway, with my vision hazy I looked at the figure get out of the car and head my way. In my drunken state I finally realized it was Pistol.

"You good baby girl?" he ask as he leaned into my face. With my unstable balance I leaned forward turning to stand but tripped in the processing causing Pistol to catch me. With my face buried in the side of his neck his sweet smelling cologne tickled my nose. "You fucked up huh? Pistol laughed as he scooped me up into his arms. "Yeah just a little." I said while showing him with my hands how much I drank. "You a mess baby girl." He said as he continued into my house, he started to lay me down on the couch when my drunken ass caused him to lose his balance and fall on top of me. Feeling his strong, muscular body on top of mine caused me to instantly get wet. I began rubbing on his arms and back as he began to start kissing on my neck up to my mouth. I closed my eyes and enjoyed the pleasure he was giving me just from his hands roaming all over my body.

Without hesitation, we pulled off each other's clothes. I wanted him so bad; I couldn't even wait for the foreplay. "Fuck me please Pistol!" I moaned out in his ear as he began to deeply finger me, causing me to quiver in pure pleasure. "Not til' I taste you first." He said before passionately kissing me on the lips. That alone made me want him even more. Pushing me back on to the couch, Pistol grabbed my legs and placed them over his shoulders as he rested his head between my legs and began to eat me out like no other. Never had I have someone suck, flick, and vibrate their tongue on my clit like he did to me. Tears of pleasure strolled down my face as he continued to feast on my pussy and let his fingers flick on both of my nipples at the same time.

"Shiiiiit!" I cried out as my whole body began to shake. I tried to scoot back, but Pistol had a tight grip on me and pulled me back onto his warm tongue. In an instant, I exploded in his mouth. I laid there trying to catch my breath, while Pistol came up for air and licked my juices off his lips.

"I'm not done with yo' ass yet!" He said, before flipping my ass over and tooted my ass up. My whole body froze as his thick tongue began to lick my pussy from the back, getting every drop of juice and made his way up to my asshole. I was shocked at how freaky he was, but I loved it at the same time.

Once again, Pistol fulfilled his mission of bringing me to the ultimate pleasure. Before I knew it, I was lying on my back with Pistols hand wrapped around my neck, gently choking me as his long and thick dick crushed my walls as he continued thrusting in and out of me. My whole body quivered every time his head continuously connected to my g-spot.

"Be a good girl and take this dick!" He commanded with his sexy voice, causing me to get wetter than before. I cried out in ecstasy as I began to squirt all over him. Never in my life had I experienced sex like this. Yet, we were nowhere near done. Pistol flipped me over causing me to be on all four on the couch. I bit down on the back of my leather couch as Pistol roughly thrusted inside of me from the back. I tried to be a G about this shit, but he felt so good that all I could do was scream loudly as he fucked me like no other. I continued to squirt nonstop until both of our bodies shook and we came in unison. I was covered in both his and my sweat as we fell laid back on the couch in each other's arms. I couldn't even move, let alone say a word. I felt like I was high off the strongest drug known to man. I laid there in a daze, amazed at what just transpired.

Gutta

After hours of contemplation of what I should do next, I decided that I was going to make things right with Krazy. I couldn't let it end like this. So I hopped in my ride and made my way to her house. As soon as I pulled up, I noticed two cars in the driveway, and the front door wide open. I could see the dim light with two figures moving around in the living room through the screen door. I parked my car on the side of the street and walked up to the screen door, only to see that fuck nigga from the Hot Boyz meeting she had a while back. He didn't have a shirt on and I could clearly see him zipping his pants up. What the fuck? I looked over to see Krazy on the couch slipping on her shirt, and I instantly knew what the fuck was going on. Rage filled my body and before I knew it i rushed into the house and tackled that nigga onto the ground as I began to punch him repeatedly in the face.

All I could see was red as I thrashed that nigga, Krazy jumped up and tried to pull me off him but I pushed her off me so hard that she slid across the floor. Instinctively I looked her way to see if she was ok but in that instant the nigga pushed me off him, we stood and squared up with each other. Fists was flying left and right. We stumbled all over Krazys living room breaking stuff as we went in at each other! Finally Krazy got us separated and held onto me like his life dependent on it. "Gutta stop please! Look at what you're doing to the house!" She screamed making me realize the damaged I caused.

I stood there with Krazy holding me, when I snatched her arms off me. "So this is the payback I get huh? I fuck a bitch so you run and fuck a nigga? The fuck type of shit is this?" I yelled angrily. Even though I just caught her fucking another nigga, in my heart I couldn't let her go. I refused to let things end like this.

"I know what I did was wrong but you can't....Naw fuck that I ain't goin' to let you choose that nigga over me!" I yelled.

<u>Krazy</u>

I stood there speechless. After all this, Gutta was once again still by my side. Even after I fucked another nigga, he still wanted me. And crazy thing is, even though he fucked another bitch, I still wanted him! I looked at Pistol, who could be nothing more than a friend in my eyes. Our eyes connected and he nodded his head like he knew exactly what I was thinking. "You don't have to choose Krazy." Pistol started. "I respect you too much and you are such a good friend to me that I wouldn't even put you in no fucked up shit like this. I'm sorry that I put you in this type of situation to begin with. So I'mma let ya'll have it." Pistol finished, before grabbing his stuff and making his exit.

After that, Gutta and I finally came to terms that it was going to be what it is. We are going to be for each other regardless of all the bullshit. As months progressed, our relationship became stronger. Ain't shit nobody can tell me about this man and vice versa. I moved back into his crib everything was back peaceful, or so I thought...

CHAPTER 4: AS IT ALL CAME TUMBLING DOWN

<u>Krazy</u>

I was knocked the fuck out sleeping in Gutta's arms as usual, when out of nowhere I felt someone punch me dead in my face! I sat up in a quickness fully awake. I was caught in shock when my eyes laid on see Cashmere standing there like she was about to kill a bitch.

"What da' fuck is dis shit! So this what da fuck you been doing huh hoe? You wait 'til Kris move to Atlanta to push up on my man!" She yelled! "Bitch calm the fuck down, I ain't even know Gutta was fucking with you!" I snapped.

"Man fuck dat shit! Run that line to another bitch!" Cashmere said before started to swing on me; in response I pushed her back, hopped out the covers and tackled her to the ground. I sat on top of her and started to punch her dead in her face. With every blow I gave her to the face, she return them by giving me blow by blow to my sides.

Gutta hopped out the bed and grabbed me off her trying to break up the fight, when Cashmere threw a punch, intend for me, but instead hit Gutta in his mouth. The whole room got quiet as she stood there, glaring at him with tears in her eyes and her chest heaving in and out. Gutta tightened his mouth as he looked at her. She backed up like she was about to run, when he instantly dropped me to the floor and lunged at her. Picking her up by her throat, Gutta started pimp smacking her ass and started to beat the breaks off her! "BITCH DON'T YOU EVER COME IN MY HOME DISRESPECTING ME!"

I sat there on the floor looking at Gutta as he started to choke and shake her, her arms look lifeless as she tried to pry his hands from around her neck. I quickly hopped up, and tried to help Cashmere pry his hands from around her neck.

"Stop it Gutta you going to kill her!" I screamed.

He quickly let go of her neck, causing her to drop to the floor. Cashmere crawled away from him gasping for air.

"How can u do this to me, I loved you, and I thought you loved me Gutta?" Cashmere said while catching her breath.

Gutta stared at her with enrage. "Bitch are you serious? Love you?" He busted out laughing like a mad man. "Bitch I just fucked wit yo' ass cause you was down to do tricks with another bitch, what nigga wouldn't like that? I need a real down ass bitch, not a scary bitch like you..."

"But…" she pleaded but was abruptly cut off by Gutta. "Shut the fuck up bitch…Do I really need to remind you that you almost got my ass killed when I took you on my last run? You claimed you could handle it but instead, you cracked under pressure. Everything about you is fake, now I see who you really are, and who you was trying to be. Why would I settle for a knock-off when I can have the original? I thought I loved you but in reality, I fell in love with the characteristics of another woman… The woman I love is Krazy and this shit between me and you is dead! So get the fuck up, wipe the blood off yo' face, and get the fuck out my crib!"

"Are you fucking serious Gutta? How are you going to love someone that's with another nigga! Everybody knows she will always be with Kris and you just stupid enough to think that she wanna be with you and actually love you back?" Cashmere laughed. "Nigga Please!"

"You know what Cashmere, that shit really don't have shit to do with you...So get the fuck out before I throw yo' dumb ass out." Gutta commanded.

<u>Krazy</u>

I stood there in disbelief that the woman that Gutta has been with was Cashmere! She stood up and wiped the blood and tears off her face. She slowly walked to the door, before turning around and giving me a cold glare. I could feel the hate radiating off of her. Without another word said, she made her exit. That look she just gave me let me know that this shit wasn't over.

A year passed after the incident with Cashmere, and me and Gutta's relationship had no limits. Everything about Kris faded away. Although I thought about him at times, it's been three years since I heard from Kris. So I figured he was either locked up or dead. I can't even say locked up because I tried to find him in every police department in Atlanta. Yet they all ended up saying the same thing "no one is here by that name." So I just took it as a lost cause and decided to move on. Kris was my past, and Gutta was my future.

Everything seemed so right when I was with him. I used to think that Kris was the one for me and that he was the only one on this miserable earth that could handle and understand me. But I was wrong! Gutta knew me better than Kris ever did; he treated me more like a woman, rather than a partner. Everything was going smooth as far as our relationship goes, but due to our relationship drama, our plan to take over The Street Legends was put on a major hold. I could tell that Gutta was getting frustrated with the failure in executing our plans, so to make up our absence I did some much need research.

I found out that the Street Legends owned a business office in downtown Detroit. Their main business was a record company that had many well-known Detroit rappers and singers, signed under them. Luckily, they were looking to hire a new personal assistant. I pulled a few strings and got the job and it was arranged for me to start work a week from today. Gutta seemed to be relieved that this mission was soon to be over and that he could finally get the justice his mother deserved.

The plan was for me to get close enough to the leader and get him alone so Gutta can come in for the kill. We found out that the one who was calling all the shoots was a guy named Isaac. The same one who was also around when Gutta's mother was murdered. He was her number one soldier, and was the only one, other than Gutta, that was allowed being by Frankie's side. So when she died, he mysteriously took over. There was no doubt about it, that Isaac killed Gutta's mother! If we took him out of the picture, the rest of the camp would fall, making it easy for us to come in and kill them all.

Gutta

The day finally came for Krazy to start working at the record company and I must say she looked fly as fuck to be a personal assistant. I snuck a couple of glances in as she made her exit from my car and made her way to the building. She had on a white V-neck blouse with a black pencil skirt, and her 6-inch pumps. I watched as she turned around before entering the building, winked at me and blew me a kiss. I waited until she disappeared in the revolving doors of the building before I pulled off heading back to the crib.

Low and behold was Cashmere sitting on my porch in some sweats and a wife beater. She looked like she was ready for war. I calmly got out of the car and tried to keep my cool, but this bitch haven't been here for a long while and I couldn't understand what made her think she could bring her ass to my crib after our last encounter. "Do you need something? Cause if not you trespassing on private property" I stated as I walked onto the porch. "No...I wanted to talk to you". She stammered with tears in her eyes like she was about to cry. I sighed deeply annoyed before replying "Talk to me about what?"

Cashmere sighing heavily before answering, "I wanted to talk about us and how..."

"There is no us!" I said, cutting her off. "So you really just going to give up on the years we spent together, all that history just for that random bitch?" Cashmere yelled. "Well thanks to yo mimicking ass I known her for three years" I laughed "Look, that shit ain't funny, I was being myself the whole time I was with you." Cashmere said, getting a full blown attitude.

"Naw sweetheart you was being a copy of what you wish you could be. So if there's nothing else I would appreciate it if you get off my property." I stared at her with a blank face.

"Gutta please think about this, seriously she ain't who you think she is. I'm telling you I've known her for a long time and she ain't really in love with you. She is just using you for the moment 'til Kris get back. That's how it's always been. You think this is the first time Kris went out of state?" Cashmere pleaded.

"To be honest Cashmere I don't give two fucks about that nigga." I spat, fully annoyed with this conversation. "Well you should because he got her wrapped around his finger, and when he finally come back... All he have to say is leave that nigga and she will do just that." Cashmere continued. "That nigga ain't coming back and if he does we will be long gone!" I snapped in anger.

"No Gutta can't you fucking get it? Where ever she go he can find her it's like they are attracted to each other, he will track you down for what is his and he won't rest till she back in his presence." Cashmere explained, causing me to laugh in response.

"Cashmere let's get this thing straight, Krazy ain't going nowhere and Kris can come anywhere he want and when he does I got something for him, if you know me you know one thing I fight for mines, and any nigga wanna test me, they can go right ahead cause I'm a different breed of man. And if she want to get back with the nigga shit, then let her. I don't give a fuck!"

"But I don't understand why you would want to go through all that when we can work out our problems and fix it?" Her annoying voice continued filling my ears. "Cause BITCH it ain't worth fixing!" I yelled.

"But...." She cried. "Look, I ain't bout to get into it with you today, not any day! Get the fuck over it! We done, nothing is about to change that, so those tears that you crying really ain't affecting me, I can give two fucks if you crying right about now. I know you have other nigga's checking for you, so do you aight." I concluded the conversation as I walked past her into the house, locking the door behind me.

Krazy

I walked into the main lobby and up to the clerk's desk. I informed the clerk that I was the new employee for the assistant position. She politely told me that I would be working under the head boss and that he would be on the 34th floor waiting for me. I smiled at her before saying thanks and heading towards the elevator. Once I made it to the 34th floor I walked up to the double doors which led to the main office. I looked at the gold plated name tag on the side of the office door that said Isaac Walton. I thought about everything Gutta and I went through just to get to this point. We are finally going to be able to knock off the head boss of the Street legends gang.

I pushed open the door and there stood Isaac looking out the window sipping on some scotch. He turn around and looked into my eyes. I stood there in a trace because something about his eyes was so familiar; I shook it off and walked up to him extending my hand to introduce myself.

"How are you doing today sir? I'm Simone; I'm going to be your new assistant. "Hello Simone glad to meet you" He smiled as he shook my hand.

"Today I just need you to clear my schedule, and let all my clients know that their appointments will resume tomorrow. I have a family reunion I have to attend today at three O' clock." He continued.

"Will that be all sir?" I asked politely. "Yes that will be it, and stay by the phone if I need you." I replied. "Yes sir" I said before walking out of his office, and heading to my desk.

I started to contact all his clients like Isaac directed, and then started to thumb through some paperwork trying to get the whole scoop on him. I found out that Isaac was the oldest of three brothers, and that they all were living in the surrounding areas of the downtown area. I pulled up all their addresses and wrote them down on my notepad. I also looked up where their family reunion was being held and that's when it hit me. Me and Gutta could take them out today!

I quickly texted Gutta the location where Isaac would be and told him we could do it tonight before the reunion ended, but he told me not to worry that he had it covered. I looked at the text message with confusion.

I know he had this revenge thing on his mind for years, but something just didn't sit right with me. The plan seemed too rushed and not very thought out. I text him back telling him to wait till I got off work but I never got a response. I slowly slipped my phone into the top drawer just in time as Isaac walked out his office and gave me a smile before heading towards the elevator. I sat there and watched him as the elevator doors closed. I stood up and tiptoed into his office.

I stood there, only to see what seemed like a police evidence room. All over the wall was photos of Gutta and I with permanent marker lines connecting us to each hit that we have done over the years. There was even pictures of us at Gutta's crib! I become enraged when I saw pictures of us have sex blown up on the wall. This mothafucka' was sick but he was smart since he knew we was coming for him. He knew who I was before I even I walked in the door! I had to get the fuck out of here!

Without hesitation, I rushed to leave Isaac's office but when I opened the door, there he standing there, looking down at me with a menacing grin that seem so familiar that it scared me. I never been so scared in my entire life.

"So my pet I see you figured me out" He said "So what you going to do with me?" I asked coldly. Isaac laughed like a mad man. "Nothing at all, we are just going to wait and see how this play out my pet." He said as he swiftly shut the office door and locked it.

<u>Gutta</u>

I walked along the shore of the Detroit river as the Princess boat floated along with the noise of happy family members partying their ass off. I laughed to myself thinking that this shit would finally be over and that their ass wouldn't even know what hit them. I planted a bomb on the boat hours before the guest arrived and all I had to do is wait until the boat was far out to trigger it. As the sky began to darken, I took in the cool air and pressed the send button on my phone and BOOM!

The boat blew up into flames. All you heard was screams of horror and it sent chills of pleasure and satisfaction up and down my spine. I smiled as I threw the phone in the water before walking off. Bystanders stood there on the waterfront in fear as the boat burned to ashes. I could hear the sirens getting closer and closer by the minute. Yet I walk slowly to my car when my phone started to go off. Krazy's number traveled across the screen, I quickly answered the phone ready to be greeted by the voice of my young thang, but was taken by surprise when I heard the voice of a man.

"So I take it you thought you took me out the game huh?" The man asked sarcastically. "Who the fuck is this?" I urged the man to reveal his identity. "Aww Gutta I'm so hurt you don't remember my voice, well then again you were young at the time so it's only right that you forgot." He chuckled in response. Searching through my thoughts it finally hit me "Isaac!" I yelled into the phone.

"Now you caught on, I knew you were smarter than what you put on! You must have thought you had everything figured out huh?" He continued. "Where's Krazy?" I asked, cutting him off. "Oh you mean yo' little bitch?" He laughed. "If you do anything to hurt her I swear…" "You swear what you little punk bitch? You ain't in the best position right now to be sending threats. See that's what's wrong with you little nigga's today. Ya'll think you know everything about the game and you always mix a bitch up with yo' shit. So let me tell you this, you got twenty minutes to get over here or yo little bitch is dead! It's your choice Gutta. Is the throne that yo' mother and your grandfather work so hard to put together worth this little bitch? Choose wisely my son." He said before hanging up in my face.

I sprinted down each block trying to reach the building where Isaac was located. My mind raced with thoughts of what he could be possibly doing too Krazy right now. As his words lingered in my head, my heart beat rapidly but ached at the same time because Krazy was everything to me. She was someone that could not be replaced. She was one of a kind; her presence alone would make any nigga squirm with fear. She stood elite to any other females, and also was a great addition to my lifestyle. She was my lover and my partner with looks and actions that can kill.

By the time I made it to the building, the whole downtown and the waterfront was filled with police officials, I ran into the building and saw that everyone was gone! I walked past the clerk's desk and saw her spread across the counter dead. Blood was splattered all over the computer monitor showing that whoever did this shot her from behind. Seeing that I knew Isaac wasn't fucking around anymore, this nigga is beyond crazy if he just offed his employee like that.

My stomach churned as I hopped into an elevator filled with a pile of dead co- workers and security guards. The whole elevator ride to the 34th floor reeked of piss and blood, causing my nostrils to burn. When I finally made it, I ran through the double doors and straight into Isaac's office only to see Krazy on her knees with tears streaming down her face. Rage instantly filled my body as I took in her face she was so badly beaten that her face was unrecognizable! Isaac stood behind Krazy with his chrome 9mm resting on the back of Krazy head. He looked at me with a menacing smile with blood lust filled eyes.

"Aight Isaac, I'm here now so just let Krazy go!" I said. "Aww, we were having so much fun together." He said as he grabbed a handful of Krazy's hair causing her to shriek in pain.

"I said let her go!" I pulled out my gun, aiming it at his head. "Now, now son, let's not be too harsh I was just having some fun!" Isaac chuckled. "I ain't yo' son you twisted mother fucker!" I spat. "On the contrary, that's precisely who you are! See your mother never could get off her high horse to admit that she slept and got impregnated by someone of a lower social status, but Shakeer I am unmistakably your father." He explained.

In disbelief I yelled. "You a fucking lie! My mother would never be involved with a sick mother fucker like you! You have no loyalty or respect for the game!" Isaac laughed. "Wow you are definitely your mother's child, she said the exact words to me the day you was born. But sorry to disappoint you but my blood runs through your veins boy! Take a look for yourself." He pointed at the full length mirror.

I stood there for a moment before walking past all the photos of Krazy and I made, and stood in front of the mirror. I stood there looking at my reflection when Isaac walked behind me, dragging Krazy every inch of the way. Our eyes, our mouth, our height was identical! There was no denying that this man's blood ran through my veins! My eyes wander down to Krazy's reflection as she stayed on her knees tugging at Isaacs hand to let her hair go. In that instant moment, I turned around and stared Isaac straight in his eyes. I looked at this man whose eyes were identical with mine, yet it had no glimpse of life left in them.

Choking out the words, I asked him the question that I've wanted to ask him for years. "Did you kill my mother?" "Don't ask questions you already know the answer to son." I cringed at the word son. "Why?"

Isaac tossed Krazy at my feet while quickly aiming his gun at me, while he walk backwards towards the window. I stooped down cradling Krazy into my arms while still keeping my gun and eyes on Isaac as he open his mouth to explain.

"You see Shakeer, you mother was the key to the Street Legends gang. With your grandfather locked up in prison and her being the only child, the throne was forced into her lap. Without an heir to the throne the empire that was passed down through the generations and would stop right with her. The honorable thing, fuck that, the right thing your mother could have done, was sworn the empire to me. But instead, she named you the next in line with the title that was rightfully mine! Without me there would be no you, so only naturally I took her out and took what was rightfully mine in the first place!" He laughed.

Scenes of the night my mother was killed flashed through my head as Isaac laughed outrageously. All of this over a fucking title that was a burden to my mother. Anyone that knew my mother would know that she never wanted this lifestyle but you can't help the family you are born into, so she sucked it up and did what she had to do! And this sick bastard killed her for making an obviously good reason not to give him power! I shook my head in disgust when I cocked my gun and rose to my feet. I stood in front of Krazy shielding her before saying my last and final words to my mother's killer.

"You took my mother from me, and disgraced our family business! And today you will finally pay retribution to the pain and agony you caused me, as well as others!"

"Oh am I? Let's see if all that training your mother put you through was worth that bitch fucking time boy! I say you have exactly five minutes to kill me before the cops arrive since that pathetic clerk of mine decided to be such a nuisance." He gleamed.

In that split seconded Isaac and I both let off our rounds, bullets ripped through my leg and arm, as my bullets hit every vital organ in that man's body! The pain was unbearable but the deed was done,

Isaac was sprawled out on the floor in a pool of his own blood and the satisfaction crept all over my body.

<u>Krazy</u>

Weakly, I got off my knees and went to Gutta's side; wrapping his arms around my shoulder I assisted him while we made our way out the office and onto the elevator. My heart was racing because I knew that it was only a matter of time before the police got there. We got to the lobby when sure enough the police had the whole building surrounded! We instantly stopped dead in our tracks and rushed back into the elevator where Gutta pressed the basement button.

"Gutta if we go to the basement the police is going to find us! They're going to search this bitch from top to bottom!" "I know but there is no other way!" Gutta winced in pain

I began to tear up before speaking "What the fuck you mean by that?" "Krazy when we get down there I want you to hide. I want you to hide and keep quiet and whatever you do don't come out until everyone is gone!" He commanded. "No! I'm not letting you take the wrap for this bullshit" I cried out. "Krazy get a fucking hold of yourself and open your eyes young thang! We are caught and a sacrifice has to be made!"

Tears ran down my face as we finally made it to the basement level. We rushed over to a whole bunch of tall boxes and crates where I sat as Gutta leaned up against the tallest crate. In that moment, all you can hear was the clatter of footsteps rushing across the basement level of the sky rise building, once known as the base of the notorious crew "The Street Legends". I sat there catching my breath as I heard the police sergeant yell "Put your hands up where we can see them". I look through the crack of the crates and boxes only to see the man that had stolen my heart, drop to his knees and raise his arms in defeat. How did all this come to this moment?

Tears streamed down my face as I clenched my necklace, my heart was filled with so much pain and agony. Everything that we had strategically planned has now fallen to shambles. Gutta winced in pain as they cuffed him and brutally yanked him off the ground. He limped trying to catch the officers pace when he turned around and stared right into my eyes as a single tear rolled down his face. I did just what he instructed and finally left when everything was cleared out.

6 Months Later

<u>Krazy</u>

I stood in Gutta's house packing the last remaining boxes of his things. As I folded his clothes placing them into a box, the image of the tear on Gutta face haunted me. My heart was shattered because I was so lost without him! There were so many times during Gutta's trial that I wanted to run up and yell "It was me! It was all my plan!" But I knew that Gutta would never forgive me for doing something like that.

Instead, he stood there in the courtroom and didn't even flinch when the jury found him guilty on six counts of murder in the first degree. My heart sunk at the thought that he was being charged for all the murders that occurred that day in the sky rise building! The judge sentenced Gutta life without parole and the only thing he did was turned back and smile at me as I sat in the back of courtroom.

After Gutta getting prison time and Kris still being gone without a trace, I sunk into a deep depression. There were moments where I wanted to kill myself to get rid of the pain inside me. Since that time never came, the pain never went away. Instead I came up with the conclusion that my life would never be the same. This is a dirty game we play out here in these streets and what I learned is that is no one can be trusted! People thought I was crazy before but the day I step back into the streets is going to be the day I paint these streets red with the blood of those who dare to wrong me.

I'll never forget the moments I shared with Gutta. Even if Kris stepped back into the picture, he would always be in my heart. My real love was now taken from me, so now it was time to get back to business, everyone held their own secrets, and Gutta was mine. Kris would never know of the moments we shared, and from all the fucked up shit Kris put me through, I was happy to hold onto the pleasure Gutta and I shared. I walked out of Gutta's house, locking it for the last time.

As I sat in the car and pulled out of his driveway I locked up my memories of the past and drove forward towards my future. I'll be taking my rightful place on the side of the ladies of The Hot Boyz crew, holding it down in the streets until Smooth and Kris return to take over the throne...

Kris

I sat leaned back in Sweetz passenger seat of her all black Benz with the presidential tints. I observed as Krazy pulled out that nigga Gutta's crib and was making her way down the street. Clenching my hand in a fist, I fumed with anger. Sweetz leaned over and grabbed my hand in attempts to calm me down. "I told you that bitch wasn't shit! This whole time she was with that nigga and now that he is locked up, she going to be crawling back to you. Just watch!" She said as if she was pleased by Krazy's betrayal.

Irritated, I shoved Sweetz's hand away from mine as my thoughts ran wild. I couldn't believe that Krazy had it in her to do this shit. I chuckled to myself while saying out loud. "Karma's a bitch! Hopefully Krazy will be ready for what's in store for her." I said nonchalantly before telling Sweetz to pull off. If Krazy think that I'm going to let her get away with making a fool out of me she is sadly mistaken I'm going to make her wish she never played me....

Dahlia

My red bottom heels clicked across the floor, as I walked to take my side next to my husband in the living room. As he looked out the window I gracefully handed him his glass of cognac. "Looks like everything is going as planned." I said with gleam, as my husband's pawns played right into our scheme. We both stood and watched Sweetz and Kris pulled off in her all black Benz. "Yeah, exactly like we planned. Looks like it time for phase two don't you think Princess?" He asked, calling me by my nickname. I smiled at my husband before giving him a kiss on his lips. "Of course Smooth, let phase two begin."

To Be Continued...........

Want to know who Dahlia is? Find out her story in the Hot Boyz Series Prequel *"The Streets Chose Me!"*

Available Now!

New Level. New Devil!

After finally seeking her revenge Krazy is finally on top. No longer affiliated with the Hot Boyz, she turned her life around and is living the life of luxury... with clean money that is! Now raising teens Mi'quel and Little Jake, Krazy's perfect little life is about to shatter.

With the madness that's about to unfold, will the last remaining member of the Hot Boyz stay on top? Or will the past haunt her and ruin everything she worked so hard for?

Find out in the next installment *Like Father, Like Son!*

Coming Soon!

Tears of a True Hustler